D0835830

The Smugglers' Caves

and Other Stories

THE
SMUGGLERS'
CAVES
and Other Stories

Illustrated by
Martine Blaney, Maureen Bradley,
Lynne Byrnes, Sally Gregory,
Jane Pape-Ettridge, Sara Silcock,
Lesley Smith, Dudley Wynn

AWARD PUBLICATIONS

ISBN 0-86163-730-5

Text copyright Darrell Waters Limited

Illustrations copyright © 1993 Award Publications Limited

Enid Blyton's signature is a trademark of Darrell Waters
Limited

First published by Sampson Low (now part of Simon &
Schuster Young Books) as *Enid Blyton's Holiday Book
Series*

This edition entitled *The Smugglers' Caves and Other
Stories* published by permission of Simon & Schuster
Young Books and Darrell Waters Limited

First published 1993
Second impression 1995

Published by Award Publications Limited,
27 Longford Street, London NW1 3DZ

Printed in Finland

CONTENTS

The
Smugglers' Caves

Bill and David were staying at their grandmother's, down by the sea.

They were very excited because Grandpa had been telling them about the old smugglers' caves round by the big cliff.

"Oh, Grandpa! Could we explore them, do you think? Should we find anything there – you know, left by the old smugglers?" asked Bill.

Grandpa laughed. "No! You'll find nothing but sand and shells and seaweed," he said. "There have been plenty of people in and out of those caves year after year. If there was anything to be found, it would have been found by now!"

"Still, it would be fun to explore

them," said David. "We could pretend we were smugglers. Come on, Bill – we'll go this morning!"

Off they went, running down the road to the big, sandy beach, and then round the sand to where the big cliffs stuck out, steep and rocky. In these were the caves.

"Oh, look – there's a whole lot of Boy Scouts on the beach," said Bill. "Gosh I wish I was old enough to be a Scout. They have such fun. I bet they're going to camp somewhere here for a week or two, and bathe, and picnic, and hike all day long! Do you think they'd let us be with them sometimes?" But when the two small boys came near the company of Scouts they didn't get much of a welcome.

"You clear off, you kids," said one of the big boys. "This is our part of the beach, see? Don't you make yourselves nuisances here."

The small boys went off, disappointed. "They could just have let us *watch* their games," said Bill. "We

8

wouldn't have been a nuisance. We could even have run after their balls for them, if they went too far."

"Oh, never mind – let's go and look for the caves," said David. "I'd rather explore them than watch boys who think we're too small to be anything but nuisances."

"Here's a cave," said Bill, and he went up to where a dark hole yawned at the foot of the cliff. "It's a big one. Let's go in."

They went into it. The floor was of soft sand, and seaweed hung down the

sides of the walls. The sea went in and out at high tide and filled the little pools at the sides of the cave.

"It's a nice cave, but not very exciting," said Bill. "I don't feel as if smugglers ever came in here, do you, David? Anyway, it doesn't lead anywhere. I mean, there are no inner caves or tunnels leading into the cliff."

"Let's find another cave," said David. So off they went to the next one. But that was very small, and they could hardly stand upright in it. They went out again into the sunshine.

Then they noticed a stretch of rugged rocks leading up to another cave in the cliff – a cave that really did look exciting. It had quite a small entrance. The boys climbed up the rocks to it and peered inside.

"It's nice and dark," said Bill. "Got your torch, David? We'll need it here."

David switched on his torch. The boys made their way inside the cave. It was really more like a big tunnel, and it led to an inner cave. David shone his

torch round. Then he gave a sudden shout.

"Bill! What's that over there? Look!"

Bill looked over to the corner into which David's torch shone. Well hidden, there were what looked like sacks and boxes. Gracious! Had they suddenly hit on some old smugglers' stores after all?

"Make sure those Boy Scouts aren't anywhere about," said David. "We don't want them to interfere in this.

11

This is *our* discovery, see?"

Bill went to the outer entrance of the tunnel-like cave. He peered out. No, there were no boys about. But wait a bit – wasn't the sea a good bit nearer now?

He called to David. "Hey! I think the tide's coming in pretty fast. Will it reach these caves, do you think? We don't want to be caught."

"Yes. I think it *will* reach them – and then we shall be stuck here for hours," said David. "Blow! Just as we have found treasure, too! I don't like going off and leaving it here, with all those Scouts about. They're pretty certain to come nosing round these caves, and then they'll find it, too."

"Well, we can't possibly take all these sacks and things down the beach with us," said Bill. "Won't it be all right to leave them here, David?"

"No. If *we* can find them, somebody else easily can!" said David. "I'm surprised nobody has spotted them before. I know what we'll do, Bill."

"What?" said Bill.

"We'll drag them to that place halfway up the cave wall," said David, pointing. "Do you see, there's a kind of big hole there? It may have been a proper hidy-hole once for smuggled things. I think we could drag everything up there and hide it well. We could drape some seaweed over the hole."

It was difficult to drag everything up to the hole. The boys did not stop to open the sacks or boxes, for they were

so afraid of being cut off by the tide. They managed to drag them into the hole at last, and then they hastily arranged big fronds of seaweed over the 'treasure' to hide it. When they had finished they were sure no one could possibly see it.

They slid down to the cave floor. They went cautiously to the outer entrance and peered out. They would just have time to run round the edge of the cliff before the sea was swirling all round it!

"There are the Scouts, look – in the next cave but one!" said Bill. "I wonder what they want. They're yelling to each other rather crossly. Somebody's done something silly, I should think."

14

"Well come on – let's go before they yell at *us!*" said David. The two small boys ran round the foot of the cliff, wading through a shallow stretch of water in one place. They were only just in time! The tide would soon be right up the cliff – and into some of those caves.

"The Scouts will get caught if they don't look out," said Bill.

"Oh, they're big enough to swim if they get caught by the tide," said David. "Or they might even dare to climb up the cliffs!"

They went home to dinner. They told Grandpa about their exciting find, but he only laughed.

"Go on with you!" he said. "Telling me you've found smugglers' treasure in those caves! Why, I've been in and out of them thousands of times when I was

15

a boy. You don't suppose you could find what I didn't do you?"

"Well, but, Grandpa," said Bill, "we really and truly *did* find treasure. At least – we didn't open the sacks because we didn't have time – but what else could be in them but old forgotten treasure?" Grandpa just laughed again. It was most disappointing of him. The boys decided not to say any more. It spoilt things if grown-ups laughed at them.

After dinner they slipped out again, hoping that the tide would soon go down and that they could once more go to the cave – and, this time, undo the 'treasure' and see what they had got!

They waded round the foot of the cliffs and came to the stretch of rocks that led up to their cave. They were soon hauling the treasure out of its hidy-hole to the floor below. "It's a jolly good thing we put it up where we did or it would have got soaking wet," said Bill. "The sea came right into the cave!"

16

They began to open the sacks – but what a surprise they got! There was no 'treasure'! One sack was full of cups and plates and knives and forks! Another one had tins of food in it, and big loaves of bread, and about three dozen buns! One of the boxes had cricket stumps and balls in! What a very extraordinary thing!

17

"This isn't smugglers' treasure!" said Bill in dismay. "But what is it? And why is it here? Who does it belong to?"

"I say – do you think it belongs to the scouts?" said David in rather a small voice. "It's rather the sort of things they'd bring away to camp with them. I don't think we'd better undo any more."

The boys stared at one another in dismay and fright. Had they meddled with the Scouts' belongings? How *could* they have thought they had found smugglers' treasure when they knew the sea swept in and out of that cave! How silly of them. No wonder Grandpa had laughed.

They were disappointed and miserable. "We simply shan't dare to say a word about this to the Scouts," said Bill, his voice trembling. "They'd skin us alive!"

"Let's go before they discover us here with their things," said David. So they crept out of the cave and made their way along the foot of the cliffs again.

And they bumped straight into a meeting of the Scouts!

"I tell you I *did* put the things into one of the caves!" a red-faced Scout was saying. "I did! Even if the sea had gone in, surely it wouldn't have swept *everything* out!"

"Well, not a single thing is there," said the Scout-leader. "And here we are, come to camp, with our food, crockery, knives and forks, everything gone! We were idiots to dump our things down like that. We should have set up camp and unpacked straight away instead of fooling about."

"I suppose there's nothing for it but to go back home," said another Scout,

19

looking very blue.

Bill and David couldn't help hearing all this. They felt dreadful. It was their fault that the Scouts hadn't been able to find their things – it would be their fault if they had to give up camping and go back home.

Bill pulled David. He was scared and wanted to get back home. But David was made of stronger stuff, and besides, he was older. He suddenly walked straight up to the Scout-leader, his face scarlet, and spoke to him.

"I'm awfully sorry – but we stuck your goods into a hidy-hole halfway up a cave-wall," he said. "A good thing we did, too, or they would have been soaked by the sea. You will find them in the cave quite safe."

"You wretched little nuisances!" cried a Scout. "You want a good telling off!"

"No, he doesn't," said the leader. "It was a jolly good thing he found our sacks and boxes and put them out of reach of the sea – and it can't have been an easy thing to walk up to us

and confess it all, not knowing what we'd do to him. He's a good youngster, and I won't have him yelled at."

There was a bit of grumbling, but nobody else shouted at Bill and David. "You come along and show me which cave the things are in," said the leader to David. "We seem to have forgotten even which cave we used!" Bill and David took the Scouts to the cave.

21

They were pleased when they saw all their goods. "Now we can camp all right," said a tall Scout. "Thank goodness these kids had the sense to drag everything out of reach of the water."

"We thought it was smugglers' treasure," explained Bill, with a red face. But the Scouts didn't laugh. The leader clapped him on the back.

"You'll make a good Scout one day," he said. "You ought to join the Cubs, you know, you and your brother. Would you like to watch us camping? You can come to breakfast tomorrow with us if you like."

22

Well, what do you think of that? The two boys beamed all over their faces.

"Oh, thanks a lot!" said David. "We promise not to make ourselves nuisances."

They didn't. They made themselves so useful that the Scout-leader said he really didn't know what they would do without them. And one night he even let them sleep in a tent with some of the others.

And now, as you can guess, Bill and David are both good Cubs. Are *you* a Cub or a Brownie? I'm sure you will be if you get the chance.

Billy-Bob's Coconut

Once Billy and Belinda saw that a fair had come to their village. It was a fine fair, with all kinds of roundabouts and swings set up in the big field at the end of the village.

Mother said she would take Billy and Belinda. So they put on their hats and coats and scarves, and off they went to the fair.

"I shall have a ride on the roundabout," said Billy. "On that animal roundabout, I think. I shall choose a giraffe. Which animal will you choose, Belinda?"

"A duck," said Belinda. So they both got on the roundabout when it stopped. There was Billy high up on an enormous giraffe with a long neck, and there was Belinda on a small duck that wobbled from side to side as the music played. Round and round they went – it was great fun.

Then they wanted a slide on the slippery-slip. So they gave a man twenty pence, and he lent them a mat each to slide down on. They climbed up some steps, put their mats at the top of the slippery-slip, and then slid down it. Oh – what fun that was!

They did that again – and then they went on the roundabout again. Mother had given them each as much as three

pounds to spend, so they really did have a good time. At last Billy had only forty pence left and Belinda had only twenty pence.

"When you've spent that, we must go home," said Mother, "It's nearly tea-time."

"I shall spend mine on having a throw at those coconuts," said Billy, who rather thought he would be a good shot. So he gave the girl his twenty pence and she handed him three wooden balls to throw at the coconuts at the back. He threw one hard. It missed. He threw

another. It just touched a coconut.

"That was quite a good shot," said Mother. Billy aimed very carefully with his third ball. He threw it hard – and it hit a coconut right off its stand. Billy was so pleased.

The girl picked it up and gave it to him. "Can I eat it when I get home and give Belinda some too?" asked Billy.

"I'm afraid not," said Mother. "Coconut isn't good for children. It gives them a pain."

"Oh, Mother! Then what can I do with my coconut? It will be wasted," said Billy sadly.

"Oh no, it won't," said Mother. "You can hang it outside your bedroom window, with a hole in each end, and the tits will simply love it. They will feast on it all the winter through, and be your friends."

"Oh, I really should like that," said Billy, pleased. "I'll hang up my coconut by my window."

"I'd like a coconut, too, to hang by *my* window," said Belinda at once.

27

"Well, you've got twenty pence left. Get some of those wooden balls to throw, and you may knock a coconut down as well," said Billy. So Belinda gave her last twenty pence to the girl, and took the three balls. But, you know, she threw very badly indeed.

The first ball hit poor Billy on the back! It didn't really hurt him very much, but he felt rather angry.

"Can't you see the difference between me and the coconuts?" he said to Belinda. Belinda frowned, and threw her second ball. This time it hit the girl who gave out the balls!

"Really, Belinda!" said Mother. "You must *look* where you are throwing! Now do be careful of your last ball."

"I'm going to get out of the way," said Billy and he stood yards away. Belinda threw the ball. It went high into the air, and dropped down nearly on top of her own head.

"You're a dreadful thrower!" said Billy in disgust. "A waste of money, I call that."

"I haven't got a coconut," wailed

Belinda. "I want some more money."

"Well, you can't have any more, Belinda," said Mother firmly. "Firstly, because you're acting like a baby and you know I never give you anything then. Secondly, because you've used up all your money. And thirdly, because I've none left in my purse, anyhow."

Billy felt sorry for Belinda. "Look, Belinda," he said. "I'll spend my last twenty pence on some more balls and *I'll* throw them and get you a coconut to take home."

So he paid for the three balls and aimed very carefully. But not one of them hit a coconut at all. Billy was very sorry.

"Now we *must* go home," said Mother. "Didn't we have a lovely time? Cheer up, Belinda. The world isn't coming to an end because you haven't got a coconut!"

So Belinda cheered up; but when they got home and Mother knocked a hole in each end of the coconut and then threaded string through the holes to hang the nut up by Billy's window, Belinda was very sad.

"I want some birds at my window too," she said. "I don't see why Billy should have all the birds. I love them too."

Well, the birds *did* come to Billy's coconut. They came all day long! There were great-tits with black heads and bright green and yellow feathers, and blue-tits with blue caps and shrill high voices. It was such fun to watch them.

"I do wish I could have the birds at my window," said Belinda a dozen times a day to Billy and Mother. And then one

31

day Mother said something exciting.

"Belinda, if you really want birds by your window, you have something in your own garden that they will love to eat if you hang it up on string."

"Oh, Mother, what?" cried Belinda.

"Come and see," said Mother. She and Belinda went down the garden and Mother pointed to the big old heads of Belinda's giant sunflowers. "Look," said Mother. "Those old sunflowers of yours have made heaps of seed in their big fat middles. The finches and the sparrows love those. Shall we cut one

32

down and hang it up for you?"

"Oh yes!" cried Belinda joyfully. So they cut the biggest one down, and Mother put some string round it and hung it up by Belinda's window.

And now *Belinda* has birds all day long at her window too – not the same ones as Billy, but sparrows and chaffinches and greenfinches, and sometimes a shy bullfinch with its black velvet head and deep red chest. Oh, Belinda has plenty of bird-friends now!

Can you get a coconut or an old giant sunflower head? If you can, hang one by *your* window! You'll have just as much fun then as Billy and Belinda do!

Fly-Pie

There was once a big cat called Paddy. He was black and white, and had enormous whiskers. He was a great mouser – and alas! he caught birds too.

But very soon the birds in the garden began to know Paddy, and to fly away as soon as he came near. The mice feared him, and ran to the fields. Even the rats wouldn't come into the garden. So Paddy couldn't catch anything at all.

He didn't really need to catch birds or mice, because his mistress fed him well. Three times a week she bought fish-scraps and boiled them for Paddy – and every day he had fresh milk and bacon rinds and scrapings of puddings, so he had plenty to eat.

But he loved catching birds and mice. One day he sat in the garden looking up into the blue sky – and up there, flying high, he saw hundreds of birds! Far more than he ever saw in the garden, thought Paddy.

He sat and watched them. They were swallows with curved wings and forked tails. You can see them any day in the summer and early autumn, if you look up into the sky.

"If only I could get those birds down here!" thought Paddy. "Tails and whiskers, what a fine feast I would have!"

He went to visit Kirry, the little pixie who lived under the hedge at the bottom of the garden.

35

"Kirry, what do those birds up in the sky eat?" he asked. "Do they nibble the clouds for their dinner – or eat a star or two?"

Kirry laughed loudly. "Those are swallows!" he said. "And they certainly don't eat the clouds or the stars – they catch flies all day long!"

"Oh, *flies!*" said Paddy, and he began to think. "Do they ever come down to earth, Kirry? There are such a lot of them up there."

"No – the swallows hardly ever come down to earth," said Kirry. "Only when they want mud for their nests, you know, and that's in the springtime."

"I wish I could get them down here," said Paddy. "I'd like to see them."

What he *really* meant was that he'd like to catch and eat them. But he didn't tell Kirry that, because Kirry loved the birds.

"Well – you won't get the swallows down here unless you give them as many flies as they can catch up there!" said Kirry.

"Oh," said Paddy, and he began to think hard. "Kirry," he said, "if I catch you a lot of flies, will you make me a fly-pie please? And send a message to the swallows to ask them to come down to tea here and eat the fly-pie?"

"Well, that's very kind of you, Paddy," said Kirry, pleased. "Yes – I'll certainly make a fly-pie for you."

So for the next few days Paddy caught flies instead of mice or birds! There were a great many of the noisy bluebottles about just then, and many Daddy-long-legs, which the grown-ups hated because their grubs ate the roots

of plants. So Paddy had a fine time catching these flies, and soon Kirry had enough to make a big fly-pie for the swallows.

He sent a message to the birds. "Please come down to tea tomorrow. There is a big fly-pie for you!"

The swallows twittered in the greatest excitement "Fly-pie! Fly-pie! Did you hear that? We'll go and eat it, eat it, eat it! We'll go and eat it, eat it, eat it!"

So they sent a message back to Kirry. "Yes! We'll all come down to-morrow to eat your nice fly-pie. Thank you very much!"

Kirry told Paddy. Paddy sharpened his claws and licked his lips. He would wait under the hedge for the swallows – and then spring out when they came, and catch dozens and dozens of them! What a feast he would have! He looked at the fly-pie which Kirry had baked. It looked fine, with a big crust on top, and a little pattern round the edge of the crust.

"They'll be here at four o'clock tomorrow," said Kirry. "Put a new bow of ribbon on, Paddy, and wash yourself well. It will be quite a party. It's so kind of you to think of fly-pie for the swallows!"

Paddy grinned to himself. Yes, he had thought of a meal of fly-pie for the swallows – but he had also thought of a meal of swallows for himself!

The next afternoon Paddy was well-hidden under the hedge. Kirry put out the fly-pie, and put ready a little knife to cut it with. Now everything was ready. Only the guests had to come.

39

But they didn't come! No – not a swallow came! Kirry waited and waited – and Paddy hid and waited too. But no swallow flew down to the fly-pie! Kirry looked up into the sky. It was quite empty of birds! Not a swallow darted in the air up there. It was very, very strange.

"Paddy!" called Kirry. "It's funny – but all the swallows have gone. I can't see a single one!"

Paddy came out, swinging his tail angrily. "*Gone!*" he said. "What do you mean, 'gone'? Just when I was looking forward to a good meal, too!"

"A good meal?" said Kirry,

40

astonished. "What do *you* mean? A good meal of what? I thought the fly-pie was for the swallows!"

"A good meal of swallows, silly!" squealed Paddy, in a temper. "Are you so foolish that you didn't know that the fly-pie was only a trap to catch swallows for me?"

"Oh! You wicked cat!" cried Kirry. "No – I didn't know that at all, or I would never have made the fly-pie for you! Now see what you have done! The swallows must have heard of your wicked trap – and they have all gone! Not one is left! Maybe they will never, never come back."

Paddy felt rather scared. Certainly the swallows had gone, there was no doubt about that – and how dreadful it would be if people got to know that he, Paddy, had driven them away because of his trap!

Paddy began to slink away, ashamed of his trick. But Kirry was very angry and shouted after him, "You're a bad cat! I don't want you for a friend any more! You and your fly-pie! Here, take it – you're the only one likely to have it now!"

He threw the fly-pie after Paddy. It broke over his head – and Paddy had to spend a most unpleasant half-hour licking the fly-pie off his thick black-and-white fur. Well, it served him right!

As for the swallows, they hadn't heard about the trap at all! You see, a cold wind had begun to blow the night before, and the chief of the swallows had decided that it was time to leave our country and fly to warmer countries far away!

So, with many twitterings, the swallows had gathered together, and then, with one accord, they had risen into the air and flown to the south! They would come back again in the spring – but Paddy didn't know that!

He just sat licking the unpleasant fly-pie off his fur, thinking, "Well, never again will I try a trick like this! No, never again."

The Voice
in The Shed

The new gardener wasn't at all nice. The children didn't like him a bit. "He shouts at me," said Ann. "Even if I'm only just walking down the path he shouts at me."

"And he told me he'd put my wheelbarrow on his bonfire if I left it out in the garden again," said John.

"And today he said we weren't to go into the shed any more," said Peter. "Why, we've *always* been allowed in the shed, ever since we can remember. It's our shed, not his."

"Does he think we'll break his tools or something?" said Ann. "We shouldn't. Anyway, they are mostly Daddy's tools, not his."

"I shall tell Daddy I don't like him,"

said John.

But Daddy only laughed. "Old Mr Jacks let you do anything you liked."

"Mr Jacks was nice," said Ann. "I liked him. He gave me strawberry plants for my garden."

"This new man, Mr Tanner, is a very good gardener," said Daddy. "Much better than old Jacks was. Maybe he thinks you children will run over his seed-beds or something. Keep out of his way."

But they couldn't very well keep out of Mr Tanner's way, because, after all, they had to play in the garden – and, except for Sundays, Mr Tanner was always there, keeping a look-out for them.

45

He ordered them off whenever he came across them. He grumbled if they dared to pick anything. But he was crossest of all if he caught them in the garden-shed.

"You're not to go in there," he stormed. "How many times do I have to tell you? I keep my things in there and I'm not having a lot of children messing about with them. You keep out."

"But we've *always* played in the shed if we wanted to," said John, boldly.

"Well, you won't any more," said Mr Tanner, disagreeably. "I'll lock it, see?"

He not only locked it, he frightened Ann and Peter very much. He caught

them peeping in at the shed window one day and he yelled at them so crossly that they almost fell off the water-butt in fright.

"You be careful," he said. "I'm going to put someone in there to scare you out! See? You be careful."

"Who?" asked Ann, fearfully.

"Ah – you wait and see," said Mr Tanner. "I'll have my Someone there very soon – and won't he chase you when you come messing around!"

Ann and Peter didn't like this idea at all. Who was this horrid Someone? Ann dreamt about it at night, and told John. He was the oldest of the three and he laughed.

"It's only something that Mr Tanner has made up to scare you," he said. "He hasn't got a Someone."

But Ann and Peter didn't believe John. They were quite sure that Mr Tanner was horrid enough to keep a strange Someone in their garden shed to scare them away. They didn't go near the shed after that.

"You shouldn't scare my sister and brother like that," said John boldly to Mr Tanner. "It's wrong."

"You get away," said Mr Tanner, in his surly voice. "I'll do as I like. Pests of children you are. I never did like a place with kids about."

John went off. He was angry. How dare old Tanner scare Ann and Peter? He went to call on his friend Tom, who lived just down the road. He told Tom all about it.

Tom listened. "Does Mr Tanner have his dinner in that shed?" he asked.

"Yes. Why?" asked John.

"Well, I've got an idea," said Tom. "What about *us* putting a Someone in that shed – a Someone who'll scare old Tanner stiff?"

"How can we do that?" asked John, in wonder.

"Well, listen," said Tom. "You know my mother's parrot, don't you? He says all kinds of things in that funny, hollow voice of his. Couldn't we stick him in the shed somewhere and hide him? He'll talk

48

as soon as old Tanner goes in – and what a fright he'll get when he hears a voice and can't see anyone who owns it!"

John was thrilled. "But what would your mother say if your parrot isn't here at home?" he asked.

"Mother's away for a few days," said Tom. "Old Mr Polly, our parrot, won't mind where we put him so long as he has plenty of sunflower seeds to eat. Anyway, we can always go and take him out of the shed when Mr Tanner has gone at five o'clock."

So that was how old Mr Polly, Tom's parrot, came to be hidden inside the garden shed. He was put there in his big cage, with plenty of food and water. One

side of the cage was covered with a sack to hide it.

"Now then you, now then," remarked Mr Polly, in a curious hoarse voice as the boys arranged his cage in the shed. He coughed in a nasty hollow way. "Fetch a doctor. A-tish-OOOO!"

He gave such a life-like sneeze that John jumped. Tom giggled. "It's all right. He's full of silly ways and sayings. Hasn't he got a lovely voice! My word, he'll make Mr Tanner jump!"

The next day Mr Tanner saw John near the garden shed with Peter, and he spoke to them sharply. "What did I tell you? Clear off – or the Someone in that shed will get you!"

Peter ran off, looking scared. John spoke up at once.

"You're right, Mr Tanner. There *is* a Someone in the shed. I heard his voice – a deep, hollow kind of voice. I wonder you're not scared, too."

"Aha," said Mr Tanner, "what did I say? You be careful of that shed!"

The parrot in the shed coughed

solemnly. The sound came out to where
Mr Tanner stood with John. He looked
a little startled.

"There," said John, cocking his head
on one side. "Your Someone is coughing.
Why don't you give him some cough
medicine?"

"It's only the old gardener in the
next-door garden," said Mr Tanner, and
drove his fork into the ground. "You
clear off."

Old Mr Polly began to whistle a
mournful tune inside the shed.

"Hear that?" said John. "Your
Someone is whistling now. You really
have got a Someone there, haven't you?
Aren't you scared, too?"

"I told you to clear off," said Mr Tanner, looking rather uneasy. John grinned and went off, very pleased with himself.

Mr Tanner couldn't imagine where the curious noises were coming from that morning. Once he heard a voice – a deep, solemn voice. It certainly sounded as if it came from the shed. Another time he heard a cough, and yet another time a sneeze. Yet, when he went and looked into the shed there was nobody there.

John went to tell Ann and Peter what he and Tom had done. They listened in amazement. Peter laughed. "I'm glad. Let's go and take our lunch near the shed today if Mother will let us – then we can see what happens."

So they took a picnic lunch to the back of the shed as soon as Mr Tanner had gone inside to eat *his* lunch!

Mr Tanner opened his lunch packet. He was just about to take up a cheese sandwich when a hollow voice spoke loudly and solemnly.

"There's NO rest for the wicked. Ah me, ah me! Fetch a doctor!"

Mr Tanner was so startled that he dropped his sandwich on the floor. He turned round to see who had spoken, but there was nobody there.

It must be somebody outside the shed! Mr Tanner picked up his sandwich and began to eat it.

The voice began again. "See, saw, Margery daw, see saw, saw see, see saw, saw see ..."

Mr Tanner began to tremble. He dropped his sandwich again.

"Who's there?" he said in a shaky voice. "Who is it?"

"Here comes a candle to light you to bed, here comes a CHOPPER!" shouted the voice very suddenly, and gave a

53

dreadful squawk that made Mr Tanner leap to his feet in fright, half expecting to see a candle and a chopper coming at him from somewhere.

"Who are you?" cried Mr Tanner, and jumped as John came to the door of the shed. John had heard all this and was thrilled. He looked at the frightened gardener.

"Is that your Someone talking to you?" he asked. "Why do you look so afraid? It's *your* Someone, isn't it?"

Old Mr Polly took it into his head at that moment to give an imitation of an aeroplane coming down low. He always did this extremely well, and it scared

poor old Tanner almost out of his life. It even startled John. Mr Tanner stumbled over a few pots and fled out of the door into the bright sunshine. He was trembling all over.

"I can't go in there again," he told John. "You fetch out my tools for me. I'm going."

And when John gave him the few tools that belonged to him, off he went, looking very pale.

The children watched him go, feeling pleased. "His Someone came to life and frightened him!" said John, with a grin. "I'll go and get Tom and we'll carry old Mr Polly back home again. Good Mr Polly – he acted well! My word, did you hear him imitate an aeroplane?"

55

Mr Polly obligingly did it again. It was wonderful! John pulled the sacking off his cage, and the three children stood and watched the old parrot admiringly.

"What will Daddy say when he hears Mr Tanner has gone?" asked Ann.

Daddy was glad! "I've heard bad things about that fellow the last day or two!" he said. "Very bad. He isn't honest, for one thing. I'm glad he's gone. I'll get old Mr Jacks back again. He's not so good a gardener, but he's absolutely honest and trustworthy."

"Oh, *good*!" said all the children. "We do like Mr Jacks."

And back came old Mr Jacks, beaming all over his face. "Well, I'm downright pleased to see you all again," he said. "I can't think why that fellow Tanner went

off as he did. Do you know what he told me?"

"No – what?" asked John.

"He told me not to go into the garden shed!" said old Mr Jacks, with a roar of laughter. "Said there was a Voice there that frightened him away. A *Voice*! Did you ever hear of such a thing? Is there a Voice there, John? What do you say to that?"

"No, there isn't any Voice there – not now old Tanner's gone, anyway," said John, and he laughed. "He scared us by telling us he kept a Someone there, Mr Jacks – but when his Someone grew a voice he didn't like it. He ran away."

"What tales you tell!" said Mr Jacks, not believing a word. "Well, Voice or no Voice, I'm having my dinner in that shed as usual every day – and, what's more, you can come and share it whenever you like."

"Thank you!" said all three, joyfully. So they often do – but they've none of them heard that Voice again! It isn't really very surprising, is it?

Adventure
up a Tree

"Here's a fine tree to climb," said Alan to John. "Let's try this one. I should think it would rock in the wind like a ship."

"Yes – and it doesn't look *too* difficult to get up," said John. "It's jolly high, Alan. We should be able to see a long way from the top."

"Come on, then," said Alan. "I'll go first. I'm better than you at climbing. You follow the way I go."

So up he went. The tree was an oak – wide-spread and very leafy. It wasn't really very difficult to climb. John followed, and soon the two boys had found a nice broad branch, not far from the top of the tree, where they could sit and eat the sandwiches they had brought.

The wind was strong. It shook the tree, and the boys liked that. "Just like a ship swaying on the sea," said Alan. "I almost expect to hear the splash of the waves!"

The two boys were friends. They loved to go out together and find a hidy-hole of some kind. Today, it was a tree. They liked to take their tea, some chocolate and a book, and have a good read together.

"I've got a new adventure book," said Alan. "I'm in the middle of it. I'll lend it to you afterwards, John – it's really exciting!"

"I like adventure stories too," said John. "But I think I'd rather *have* an adventure than read about one. I've never had an adventure in my life ... I don't believe many people do – do you, Alan?"

"Oh, *yes*," said Alan. "And I'm sure adventures happen suddenly. Why, one might happen to us at *any* moment!"

"Pooh," said John, staring down from the tree at the quiet countryside around. "Whatever do you think could happen to us up here, this quiet afternooon? Nothing at all!"

"I can't really think of anything," said Alan. "But adventures *do* seem to happen out of nothing – at least, they do in books."

60

"Is that a bird whistling?" said John, lifting his head to listen. "I've never heard *that* song before!"

It was a flute-like whistle, rather like a blackbird's, and it sounded not very far off. Both boys listened, forgetting their talk about adventures. The whistling stopped, and then began again for a bit.

"I don't believe it's a bird," said John. "I think it's someone down in the wood." As he spoke, the boys could hear twigs cracking and the rustling of leaves as somebody pushed his way through the wood below.

"Ssh!" said Alan. "Whoever it is is coming this way. We don't want them to see us. This is our secret hidy-hole today."

The whistling sounded again, exactly the same. "Sounds like a kind of signal

61

to someone," said John. "Somebody meeting someone, I suppose."

"Be quiet – he's coming under our tree," whispered Alan. Both boys sat as still as mice. Alan was right – the newcomer was now directly under their tree. Then all at once another whistle sounded. Someone else was coming, too.

"Can you see who they are?" asked John, in a whisper. "Are they boys? Do you know them?"

Alan peered down through the branches. All he could see was the top of two heads, and each head wore a cloth cap. Then the boys heard men's voices.

"Where's Jim? He's always late! We'll wait for a few minutes, then leave a note for him."

"Right. He'll have to know what to do, and we've got no way of getting in touch except this meeting-place. What's kept him?"

There was the sound of a match striking and then the smell of cigarette smoke. The men were evidently smoking whilst they waited.

The boys whispered together. "We won't make a sound! The men might be angry if they knew we were over their heads."

"All right. Don't drop your book on them, or you'll give us away. It's slipping off the branch!"

John caught his book before it fell. The men below smoked on without a word. After ten minutes or so they got up. "I'll scribble a note," said one, and there was the sound of rustling paper. Then there was a silence. One of them was writing.

63

After that the two men went, and the boys heard their voices in the distance. They looked at one another. "It seems a bit odd, somehow," said John. "What shall we do? Go down and find the note?"

"Well – the third man might come and catch us," said Alan. "One of us would have to stay up the tree and look out for him, I think."

"You go down, then," said John. "I'll stay up here. I'll whistle if I see or hear him. Buck up."

Alan shinned quickly down the tree. He wondered if he ought to read somebody else's note – there really was something a bit peculiar about all this. The two men hadn't sounded

nice men – and why should they have a meeting-place in the wood when they ought to be working?

Alan came to the foot of the tree. He looked about for the note, but there was no sign of one. That meant the men must have hidden it somewhere – in some place where the third man would know where to look for it. Alan began to hunt about.

He lifted up a big stone. Nothing there. He parted the leaves of a bush and looked in the middle. Nothing there, either. He saw a rabbit hole nearby and put his hand down. No – nothing to be found.

"How are you getting on?" called John. "Found it?"

"No," said Alan. "I've looked everywhere. I'll just look round the tree-trunk – there might be a cranny somewhere."

He was right. There was a crack in the trunk just wide enough for him to put in his hand. He slipped it in and immediately felt paper. He drew it out. It was a single sheet torn from a notebook. Alan read what was on it.

"Bring car to l.c. gates, 3.10 sharp."

That was all there was. What in the world did it mean? What were l.c. gates?

And did 3.10 mean afternoon or early morning? Alan didn't know.

A low whistle disturbed him. "Alan! Someone's coming!" came John's guarded voice. Alan thrust the paper back into the trunk of the oak and scrambled up the tree again. The two boys waited in silence for the newcomer.

He came straight to the tree. It must be Jim, then, whoever Jim was – the one the other two had waited for. There was the rustle of paper. Jim had known the hiding-place for it and had drawn it out. There was a moment's silence. Perhaps he was now reading the message. Then there was the rustle of paper again.

After that there was only the sound of footsteps going away and twigs crackling on the ground now and then.

The boys slid down the tree. John asked Alan where he had seen the hidden paper, and put his hand into the crack to feel it. At once he felt paper, and drew out the same little sheet that Alan had seen.

But now a few more words had been added. "O.K. Have arranged for us to go to Big Harry's after."

"I don't like this," said Alan. "I shan't put this note back. I shall keep it. It's odd. I'll ask my father about it tonight."

But he couldn't, because his father came home too late that night, and Alan was in bed and fast asleep. John was awake, wondering if by *any* chance they had nearly had an adventure that afternoon. It had all ended rather tamely, for both boys had had to hurry back because they were late, and had raced through the wood and through the town to their homes.

In the morning Alan's father read the newspaper as usual. He gave an exclamation. "Well – what will happen next? Somebody set the level-crossing gates against the 3.10 train very early this morning – and when it stopped a couple of men got into the guard's van, knocked him over the head, took a mailbag and escaped. No sign of them at all!"

Alan listened, open-mouthed. The 3.10! Why, 3.10 was in that note surely? Did it refer to the train that went over the crossing in the middle of the night?

"'L.c. gates' – level-crossing gates, of course!" thought Alan. "We might have guessed. I must tell Daddy."

"Daddy," he began, but his father was looking at the clock. "Good gracious, I'm late! I shall miss my train. Goodbye, all of you!"

Alan decided to tell John before he

said anything. It was Saturday, so he was free. He did the errands for his mother and then shot off to John's. He found John in a most excited state, for he, too, had seen the papers.

"I say, Alan, that note! That was the plan made for that robbery!" began John, as soon as he saw Alan. "I've worked it all out. They shut the gates, stopped the train, and two of them knocked out the guard and robbed the van. The third man – the one the others called Jim – brought the car to the gates, so that he might take the bag and the other two men away – to Big Harry's, wherever that might be."

"Yes, I know!" said Alan, just as excited. "Golly – we were in the middle of an adventure and didn't know it. We'll have to go to the police now, John. Thank goodness I've got that note, so they'll believe us."

The police were surprised to see the two boys walking into the police station. "Well, boys, what do you want?" said the constable there.

"We've got something to tell you about the men who robbed the train – the 3.10 last night," said Alan.

"Tell away," said the policeman, getting out his notebook.

"There were three of them," said Alan, "and one is called Jim. They had a car waiting at the gates, and they have all gone to Big Harry's."

The policeman put down his notebook and stared in amazement at Alan. "How do you know all this?"

"We were up a tree near where they met yesterday," said Alan. "They didn't know we were there. They left a note in the tree and we took it. We thought it was all very odd. I meant to tell my father but I fell asleep before he came home. Here's the note."

71

The policeman whistled in surprise. He took the note and read it. He called through a door. "Hey, come here. There are two boys who know a lot more about last night's happenings than we do!"

Soon Alan was telling his tale from beginning to end. The policemen

listened. "Go out to the tree with one of these boys and see what you can find," the chief said to one man. "Cigarette ends, perhaps – or footprints."

"There *are* cigarette ends – and a match too – and footprints, but not very distinct!" said John, wishing he had been sensible enough to pick up the cigarette ends and match for himself. They were clues, of course!

"Could you boys recognise these fellows if you saw them again?" asked the chief.

They shook their heads. "No," said Alan. "We only saw the tops of their heads, you see – we were up the tree. But we saw their caps, of course. They all wore cloth caps."

"Would you know those again?" asked the chief at once.

"Oh, yes," said Alan. "We stared down at them for quite a long time! One had a navy blue cap with a tear in it."

"And one had a tweed cap, awfully dirty," said Jack. "And the third one had a brown cap, rather new, with a big

73

button on the top – brown and flat."

"I want you to stay here for a few minutes," the chief said to Alan. "The other boy can go to the oak tree with this constable and bring back anything they find. Then we will all hop over to Big Harry's. So Big Harry knows about this, does he? Well, well – I often wondered what went on at Big Harry's!"

"What *is* Big Harry's?" asked John.

"Just a place where men can sleep for the night," said the chief. "It's a pity you wouldn't recognise these three again – but if you can spot their caps that will be just as good."

John and the policeman went to the tree and collected two cigarette ends and a match. "They smoke Silk Cut cigarettes, sir," reported the constable,

when they got back to the station. "And this is a special kind of match, sir – rather big."

"Right," said the chief. "Good. Now, you two boys, I want you to come with me and do a little cap-spotting. Ready?"

Well, it was a real thrill to go in the big police car and roar down the road to the next town. Alan and John looked at one another in delight. Whoever would have thought such a thing would happen?

They came to a narrow, rather dirty street. At one end was a tall, ugly building. This was Big Harry's.

The police pushed their way into a dark, dirty hall. Pegs ran all the way down, hung with dirty coats and caps and hats. The chief shone a torch on to them.

75

"Spot the caps, boys," he said. "That one," said John, pointing to a tweed one. "And that one! That's the brown one with the flat button."

"And here's the navy one," said Alan. "There you are, sir, those are the ones."

"Thanks," said the chief. "Now we'll just find Big Harry and tell him to turn out all his boarders into the street. He won't know why and we shan't tell him! All we want to see is who takes those three caps. Then we shall know what to do!"

To the two boys enormous disappointment, they had to go back and wait in the police car. They didn't see Big Harry, frightened and blustering

when the police told him to turn out all the men who had slept there the night before. Some were still in bed! However, they were all turned out, and, grumbling and grousing, they went to fetch their coats and caps and hats.

Of course, the three thieves took their own caps – and what a shock for them when the police arrested them and charged them with the robbery of the night before! One of them was smoking a Silk Cut cigarette, and another had a box of matches on him full of matches exactly like the one found under the tree.

"Well, boys," said the chief, when the two boys were back at the police station, excited and thrilled. "You did well to spot those caps! Made our job very, very easy! Those young men will not be wearing caps for a very long time. And a good thing, too."

The boys said goodbye and left together. "What will our parents say?" said John. "How do you like adventures, Alan? We were in the middle of one yesterday without knowing it!"

"I like them very much – so long as I'm on the right side," said Alan. "I would rather catch a thief than be one. What cowards they were to attack the guard of the train like that! Gracious, John – let's have another adventure, shall we?"

"We'll look out for one," said John. And they are looking very hard. I do hope they find another soon, don't you?

Wagger Goes to the Show

"Mummy, there's to be a garden-party at the Hall, in the grounds, next month!" said Terry, coming in with his sister Alice and his dog Wagger. "Can we go?"

"There's to be all kinds of fun," said Alice. "There's a donkey to give rides, and all sorts of competitions, and swings and ice-creams. We can go, can't we, Mummy?"

"Yes, of course," said Mummy. "You must start saving up your money at once, then you will have nice lot to spend."

"And, Mummy, there's a baby-show," said Alice.

"Isn't it a pity we haven't got a baby, because then it might win a prize at the baby-show. I expect Mrs Brown's baby will win. It's the fattest baby I ever saw."

"Oh, it isn't always the fattest babies that are the best ones," said Mummy. "Well, I'm afraid you can't take a baby. You're my baby, Alice, and you're seven!"

"Let's put Alice in for the baby-show," said Terry with a grin.

"I'm not a baby," she said. "Oh, there's a dog-show too. We're going to put Wagger in for that. What sort of dog is he, Mummy".

"He's what we call a mongrel – just a mix-up of a dog. He's not pure-bred like the fox-terrier next door. He's a very ordinary, rather ugly mongrel."

"Mummy!" said both children in horror. "He's *not* ugly! He's beautiful."

"Well, darlings, you think he's beautiful because he's yours and you love him," said Mummy. "But he isn't really beautiful. His tail is too long. He's too big. His ears aren't quite right. He'd never win a prize a dog-show." Wagger looked up at the children and wagged his long plumy tail. They stared down at him, looking into his bright eyes.

"I didn't know he was a mongrel," said Alice. "I didn't know he was a mix-up dog. I thought he was the nicest dog I ever knew. I still think so."

"So do I," said Terry and he gave Wagger a stroke on his head. "And I'm going to take him to the garden-party even if all the dogs there turn up their noses at him! He'd hate to be left behind."

"Well, don't put him into the dog-show," said Mummy. "Everyone would laugh at him, he's such a peculiar-looking dog. Yes, I know he's a darling, and faithful and loving – but he *is* ugly!"

The children went out, with Wagger jumping beside them. They simply

couldn't see that he was ugly at all. "He's got the nicest eyes!" said Terry.

"And the loveliest ways," said Alice. "Does it matter so much that he's a mongrel? Oh dear – it's a shame he can't go in for the show."

"Well, he mayn't be the most beautiful dog, but he's the happiest and healthiest," said Terry. "We look after him much better than they look after their dog next door."

"Yes, we do," said Alice. "Wagger always has good meals and fresh water every day. And we bath him properly, and brush his coat well every morning. And he has a warm blanket in his basket, and lots and lots of walks all the year round."

"Wuff," said Wagger, licking Alice's hand.

"He understands every word we say," said Alice, and she hugged him. He licked her face all over.

"Don't be upset because Mummy said you were ugly," said Alice. "*We* think you're lovely, Wagger."

83

"Wuff," said Wagger happily. He wagged his long tail so fast that it could hardly be seen.

The children saved up their money that month. They ran errands and weeded the garden, and cleaned Daddy's bicycle, and whatever they were paid they put into their moneyboxes. Soon they had quite a lot of money.

"It's the garden-party tomorrow," said Alice to Terry one day. "Mummy's washed my blue dress for me. And you've got new jeans to wear."

"We ought to make Wagger look nice too," said Terry. "Let's give him a bath with plenty of soap and warm water. And we'll brush his coat till it shines."

"I wish we could clean his teeth too," said Alice.

"His teeth always do look white and clean," said Terry. "He wouldn't like you to do that. I wish we had a new collar for him. His is old and rather dirty-looking."

"Well, that won't matter," said

Mummy. "He's not going in for the dog-show, so he doesn't need to be all dressed up in new collars and ribbons. So long as he is clean and healthy, that's all that matters when you take him out with you. Get out the big plastic bowl if you want to wash him."

They bathed Wagger between them. He was as good as gold. He never made

a fuss about being washed like the dog next door did. He just stood in the warm water and let himself be soaped all over. He even shut his eyes so that the soap wouldn't get into them. He was as clever as that!

The children rinsed him and dried him. Then they took turns at brushing his thick, silky coat. It was rather curly, and it was fun to see the curls come up under the brush.

They even brushed his big ears and his long tail. He looked very fine indeed when they had finished with him. He capered about in delight, barking.

"I still think he's beautiful," said Alice, looking at him. "He's such a happy-looking dog. His eyes are so bright, and his tail is so waggy. Wagger,

you're a darling!" Wagger licked her
and pranced off again. He was certainly
a very lively dog, always ready for a
walk or a game.

Next day the children set off to the
garden-party, with Wagger at their
heels, freshly brushed. They paid their
money at the gate and ran beside the
donkey all the way round the garden
and back.

Then they had ice-creams, and
Wagger licked up all the bits that
dropped on the ground. After that they
went to have a swing, and Wagger
waited on the ground below, because he
didn't like swinging.

Then they all went to see the babies
at the show, and Alice was glad she
wasn't the judge, because she thought

all the babies were as nice as one another. Terry didn't like them so much. He said they made too much noise, and their faces were ugly when they screwed them up to cry.

Then they had another ice-cream each, and spent some money trying to fish prizes out of a pretend fish-pond with a little fishing rod. But they weren't lucky, and couldn't hook a single prize! Wagger watched solemnly, and once he wuffed as if to say "I'm sure *I* could hook a prize if I had a chance!"

Then a bell rang, and someone called out that the dog-show was about to

begin. Everyone with dogs hurried to the big tent. What fine dogs there were, to be sure. Terriers dancing about on neat little legs, Pekes, with their snub noses, looking rather haughtily around. Scotties and Sealyhams barking loudly with excitement. Really, it was all very thrilling!

"We'll go in and see the show," said Terry. "But we'd better leave Wagger outside, as we can't show him. It's a shame! Poor Wagger. He can't help being a mongrel."

They tied Wagger up outside the tent and went in. There was a ring of sawdust inside, and here people walked their dogs round and round when they were showing them. The children watched, and the judges, sitting nearby, made notes and talked in

89

low voices to each other.

Then they called out which dogs won the first prize and second prize. The fox-terrier who belonged to the family next door won second prize and got a red ticket. His owner, a big boy called Ray, was delighted.

"See, Terry," he said, as he passed him. "I've got second prize for Nobby. Pity your dog's such an awful mongrel!"

Then one of the judges got up to speak. "We have now awarded all the prizes for the various breeds of dog," he said. "But there is one special prize to come, for which any dog can be entered, whatever breed he is. This is a prize given for the best-kept and healthiest dog. Please bring your entries to the ring one by one."

So one by one the dogs were all brought up. Ray brought his Nobby too, proudly wearing the red ticket marked "Second" in his collar.

And then a dog walked into the ring all by himself! The children gasped. It was Wagger! Somehow he must have wriggled himself free and come to find Alice and Terry. He walked into the ring of sawdust, looking all round for them.

The judges thought he was entered for the competition. One put his hand on Wagger's collar and looked at his teeth. Wagger didn't mind at all. He just wagged his tail hard.

The judges ran their hands over his coat. They looked at Wagger's eyes. They lifted up his feet and felt down

his legs. Wagger barked joyfully. He thought they were making a nice fuss of him.

Wagger was the last dog in the ring. One of the judges looked round the tent and called out loudly:

"Who owns this dog? Will they please come forward?"

Rather scared, Alice and Terry went into the ring. Wagger greeted them with loud barks, licks and jumps.

"We – we didn't mean ..." began Alice. But the judge interrupted her.

"Ah, so you own this lovely dog," he said. "Well, I am pleased to say that we shall award him the prize for being the healthiest and best-kept dog in the show. His coat, his teeth, his spirits are all first-class – a very fine specimen of a dog, and most intelligent."

And, to the children's enormous surprise, one judge handed Terry a white ticket marked "FIRST" in big letters, and another judge handed Alice a new collar for Wagger, and a big box of chocolates for both of them.

"Oh, thank you," said the children, and Terry said, "But – he's only a mongrel, you know."

"Any dog can enter for this kind of competition," said the judge, smiling. "It's for the best-kept, healthiest dog – no matter what kind he is, pure-bred or mongrel. You deserve the prize for keeping your dog in such good condition."

Wagger barked and licked the judge's hand. The children turned away in delight, and bumped into Ray, who was holding Nobby on a lead.

"We've got a First," said Terry, beaming. "Oh, Ray – Wagger's got a First, and Nobby's only got a Second. I've never had such a surprise in my life."

93

"Let's go home now," said Alice. "I want to tell Mummy. Let's go quickly. And we'll give Mummy the box of chocolates, because it was she who taught us to keep Wagger so well and happy."

So they left the garden-party and tore home to tell Mummy the good news. She was just as surprised and delighted as they were. She hugged them all, Wagger too.

"We must all share the chocolates," she said. "Wagger, you look fine in your new collar. Really, you look beautiful!"

"He does, he does!" said Terry. "And he's going to have his share of the chocolates, just for one. Three cheers for old Wagger, the best dog in the show!"

"Wuff, wuff, wuff!" said Wagger, three times, and made everyone laugh. Really, he's a very clever dog, indeed!

94

The Surprising Broom

Benny and Anna had both been naughty. They had been rude and disobedient, and their mother was very cross with them.

"You are not at all nice children lately," she said. "You don't try to help me in any way. I am very angry with you. You want a good punishment!"

Now their mother hardly ever punished them, so Benny and Anna didn't feel at all upset. They didn't even say they were sorry.

"I've got to go out and do some shopping," said Mother. "You two can really do some hard work for me for a change. You can take the big broom and sweep out the yard. It is full of bits and pieces, and I haven't time to do it."

"Oh, Mother! We do hate sweeping," said Benny sulkily. But Mother for once took no notice. She picked up her basket and went out to do her shopping.

The two children looked at one another sulkily. "You have the first sweep," said Anna.

"That's just like a girl!" said Benny. "No – you're the bigger of us two. You begin first."

"Benny! Don't be mean!" cried Anna, and she smacked her brother hard. Then, of course, there was a quarrel, and in the middle of it a funny old lady came by and watched from over the yard fence.

"What's the matter?" she called.

The children stopped fighting for a moment and looked at the old woman.

"Our mother says we are to sweep the yard and we don't want to," said Benny. "It's hard work. I think Anna ought to begin as she's the bigger one – and she says I ought to because I am a boy!"

"Dear, dear!" said the old lady. "Is it such hard work to sweep a little yard like this? Well, well – if you like to give me some coins out of your money-box, I will sell you a spell that will make the broom sweep the whole yard by itself."

Well, you can guess that Benny and Anna were surprised to hear that! A spell! What fun! They ran to get their money-boxes at once. Benny had ten pence in his and Anna had twenty pence in hers. Thirty pence altogether.

They gave the money to the old woman. She picked up the broom and rubbed some yellow stuff on it,

muttering some strange-sounding words as she did so. The she smiled a funny smile, nodded her head, and went off down the road, her green eyes twinkling brightly.

The broom leaned against the fence. It grew a little head at the top and winked at Benny.

"Look at that, Anna!" said Benny excitedly. "Hey, Broom – do your work. Sweep, sweep, sweep!"

The broom stood itself up. The little head nodded and grinned. It really was a very wicked-looking head! And then the broom began to sweep.

My word, how it swept that yard! It was marvellous! It swept it far, far better than the children would have done. Anna and Benny were delighted.

"That's right! Sweep up all the rubbish!" shouted Benny, dancing about for joy. It was such fun to see a broom sweeping all by itself with nobody holding it at all.

The broom began to whistle as it swept. The little head pursed up its

funny lips and a cheery, magic-sounding tune came from them in a whistle as clear as a blackbird's.

"Sweeeeeeep, sweeeeep, sweeeeep!" went the broom all over the yard. Dust was swept up, paper was cleared into a heap, bits and pieces went into a neat pile. The job was soon done, I can tell you!

"Thank you so much, Broom," said Anna, pleased. "Now you can have a rest. You've done well."

The broom looked at Anna and then at Benny, and went on whistling its funny little tune. It didn't seem to want a rest. It swished itself over towards Anna's doll's pram, and swept it right over on to its side. The dolls fell out, and all the blankets and rugs fell

99

out too. The broom swept the whole lot over to the pile of dust.

Anna gave a scream. "Oh! You wicked broom! You've knocked my pram over! Stop sweeping away my poor dolls!"

But the dolls were now on the top of the dust-pile! Then the broom scurried over to where Benny had put his toy fort and soldiers. Crash! Over went the fort, and down went all the soldiers – and off they were swept to the dust heap.

It was Benny's turn to be angry then – but the broom didn't seem to care at all. It just went on whistling and sweeping, its little head nodding and smiling all the time.

It went to the dustbin. It swept hard

against it, and over it went. The lid went rolling across the yard with a clatter. Everything fell out of the dustbin at once!

Then the broom had a wonderful time! It swept everything up – ashes, tins, broken bottles, bits of cabbage, old tea-leaves – and what a fine pile it made! Then it swept up the dustbin too, rushed across to the lid and swept that up as well.

After that the broom went quite mad. It hopped to the kitchen door and swept up the mat there. It went inside the kitchen and swept all the saucepans and kettles off the stove. They made a tremendous clatter as they rolled across the yard to the dust-heap, with the broom sweeping madly behind them, whistling its silly little song all the time!

Then it swept the chairs out of the kitchen too, and the cat's basket as well – with the cat inside! Puss was so terrified that she didn't jump out until the basket was falling down the step. The broom tried its best to sweep her up, but the cat fled away over the fence.

"Oh, stop, stop, you wicked broom!" yelled Benny. But it was no good – the broom didn't stop. It just went on and on sweeping things out of the kitchen. When it tried to sweep all the things off the dresser, Anna was frightened.

Whatever would Mother say if she came home to find half her cups and saucers and plates broken?

"Benny! You must stop the broom!" cried the little girl in dismay.

Benny rushed over to the broom. Anna followed. Benny tried to catch hold of the handle, but the broom dodged cleverly. Benny tried again. The broom swung itself round and rapped Benny hard on the knuckles.

"Oooh!" yelled Benny. "You horrid thing! Wait until I catch you!"

But that's just what Benny couldn't do! The broom wasn't going to be caught just as it was having such a marvellous time. No, no! It was too much to ask.

So it dodged and twisted and got in some more little raps on Benny's hands and legs. Benny was so angry that he rushed round and round and round after the broom and got so giddy that he couldn't see where he was going.

He bumped right into Anna and they

both fell over, bump! The broom gave them each a good whack – and then, my goodness me, it began to sweep them up!

Over and over went the two children, rolling towards the dust-heap. The broom was so strong that they couldn't even get up! They yelled and howled but the broom took no notice. It wanted to sweep, and sweep it did!

Just as Benny and Anna rolled to the dust-heap their mother came in at the gate. At once the broom became still and quiet, and leaned itself against the fence. Its funny little head disappeared. It was a broom as good as gold.

"Benny! Anna! What in the world do you think you are doing?" cried their mother. "Get up at once. And goodness me – why have you taken all the mats and chairs and saucepans out here? Did you mean to throw them away? You bad, naughty children, what a mess the yard is in!"

Benny and Anna picked themselves up, dusty and dirty, their faces tear-stained and their hair untidy. They were both crying.

"Mother! It wasn't our fault. It was that horrid broom!" wept Anna. "It's grown a little head – and it began to sweep everything up, even us! We couldn't stop it."

Mother looked round at the broom. It had no head now. It was a good, quiet, well-behaved broom, leaning against the fence. Mother was very angry.

"I don't know how you expect me to believe fairy-tales about my broom growing a head and sweeping things out of my kitchen! It's never behaved like that with *me!* You are disgraceful children. Go straight indoors and up to bed!"

Mother went indoors with her shopping bag. The children followed her, crying. Just as they were going into the kitchen, a voice called them. They turned, and saw the old woman who had rubbed the spell on the broom.

"That broom will always be ready to sweep you up if you don't behave yourselves!" she called. "Just you be careful now!"

So they are being very careful – and all I hope is that I'm there if they begin to be bad again, because I *would* love to see that broom going mad, and sweeping up Anna and Benny, wouldn't you?

The
Old Bicycle

Peter had a long way to go to school each morning. It took him half an hour to get there, so he had to start very early.

Some of the children went to school on bicycles, and Peter wished he could too. So when his birthday came near he asked his mother if she thought she could get him one.

"Mother, couldn't I possibly have one?" he begged. "It would save me so much time. I get quite tired walking such a long way."

"Peter, you can't ride a bicycle, so it's silly to ask for one," said his mother.

This was quite true. Peter couldn't ride. He could ride Marjorie's tricycle, and he could easily pedal along in Jim's little motor-car – but he couldn't ride a bicycle.

So he made up his mind to learn. On Saturday morning he went round to Jimmy's house and asked him if he could try to ride his bicycle.

"How do you ride it without falling off?" he asked.

"Well, if I were you, I'd try putting your right foot on the left pedal first, and use the bicycle like a scooter," said Jimmy. "Take hold of the handles – that's right – now put your foot on the left pedal – yes, like that. Now, off you go. Push yourself along with your left foot, and try to get your balance."

So off went Peter round the garden, and he soon found that he could keep his balance very well like that. Then he

put his right foot across to the right pedal, and the left foot on the left pedal and tried to see if he could balance like that too, with no foot on the ground at all. He couldn't at first and over he went. But he didn't hurt himself.

He tried again and again. He had to go home when dinnertime came. Jimmy said he could come in the afternoon and try again.

Well, it really wasn't very long before Peter had taught himself to ride on Jimmy's bike, and he was very pleased about it.

"Now Mother can't say I don't know how to ride!" he thought. So he spoke to her again.

"Mother, I can ride a bicycle now. I've learnt on Jimmy's. I can ride beautifully. So may I have a bicycle for my birthday, please?"

"Well, I'll talk to Daddy," said Mother. "But bicycles are very expensive things to buy, you know, Peter, and we haven't very much money."

Mother spoke to Daddy that night, and the next day she told Peter what his father had said.

"Daddy says he can't possibly afford to buy you a bicycle," she said. "I'm sorry, Peter dear, because I know you'll be dreadfully disappointed after learning to ride – but it's no use expecting Daddy to buy you one, so don't hope for it."

Peter *was* disappointed. He didn't say a word but he went up to his bedroom and screwed up his eyes to stop any tears from coming out. After all, he was soon going to be nine and he was far too big to cry about anything.

When his birthday came his mother gave him a fine box of soldiers and his father gave him a book about aeroplanes.

"Sorry about the bicycle, old son," said Daddy. "I'd give it to you if I could, you know that. But I just can't afford it. I'm afraid you must go on walking to school."

Now that very morning something happened to Peter. He was walking to school as usual when he saw a boy coming along on a bicycle. The bicycle was small and the boy was big. Just as the boy got near to Peter, a dog ran across the road in front of the bicycle.

The boy swerved but the dog ran right

111

into him. Over went the boy with a crash on to the ground, and the bicycle fell on top of him, its wheels spinning in the air! The dog gave a yelp and fled for its life.

Peter ran to help the boy up. But the boy could not stand.

112

"I've hurt my leg," he said. "I do hope it's not broken. Can you drag me to the side of the road?"

So Peter dragged him to the side and the boy took down his sock and looked at his poor leg. "It hurts dreadfully," he said. Peter knew that it must, because the big boy had tears in his eyes. No big boys ever cried unless they really couldn't help it.

"What shall I do?" said Peter. "Where do you live?"

"Well, my father is Dr Johns," said the boy. "I'm Adam Johns. If you could possibly go to my home and catch my father before he starts out on his rounds, he could come along here at once in the car. But you'll have to be quick, because he is starting out early this morning."

"But your house is ever so far!" said Peter. "It will take me ages to get there, even if I run."

"Can you ride a bike?" asked Adam. "If you can, see if mine is all right. It doesn't look as if I smashed anything when I fell over."

"Yes, I can ride," said Peter. "I've never ridden in the road before, but I can be careful. I'll go right away now and see if I can catch your father. Goodbye!"

Peter jumped on to Adam's bicycle. "Just be careful now!" shouted Adam. "I don't want *you* to have an accident too!"

Peter was careful. He rode well to the left of the road, and didn't take any risks at all. The bicycle was just the right size for him. It seemed rather an old one, for the paint was worn off, and the bright parts were rusty. Part of the rubber of the left pedal was missing, and the right brake wouldn't work. But it was lovely

to ride a bicycle, even though it was an old one. Peter rang his bell at the corners, and at last came to Dr Johns' house. The doctor was just stepping into his car to go to see a patient.

Peter rode up, ringing his bell as loudly as possible. The doctor turned round.

"Wait a minute, wait a minute!" shouted Peter. "I've a message for you."

Then he jumped off the bicycle and

told the doctor what had happened to Adam. The doctor listened with a grave face. "What a good thing you were able to ride a bicycle!" he said. "You'd better ride to school on it this morning or you will be late. Thank you for your help. I'll go straight to Adam now."

He set off in his car. Peter rode to school being very careful indeed not to go too fast because of the broken brake.

He rode home on the bicycle too, and Mother was most astonished to see him arriving at the gate on a bicycle.

"Where did you get that from?" she asked. Peter told her.

"Mother, could I have my dinner quickly so that I can ride the bike back to Dr Johns and ask how Adam is?" he said. "Then I can leave the bicycle there and walk to school in good time."

"Very well," said his mother. "But don't gobble or you'll be ill!"

Peter soon finished his dinner. Then he went to his bookshelf and looked along his books. He thought perhaps Adam might like a book to read if he

had to rest his leg – and perhaps he would like a jigsaw puzzle to do, too.

He put a book in the bicycle basket and a jigsaw puzzle. Then off he went, ringing the bell merrily at the corners. He soon came to Adam's house. He put the bicycle in the front garden and rang the door bell.

The daily help showed him into the drawing-room, and in a moment Adam's mother came into the room.

"You must be the boy who so kindly helped Adam this morning!" she said. "Thank you very much indeed."

"How is Adam's leg?" asked Peter.

117

"I'm afraid it is broken," said Mrs Johns. "But not very badly. And as you fetched help so quickly, it was set almost at once and will soon be mended."

"I've brought Adam a book to read, and a puzzle," said Peter. "I'm really awfully sorry his leg is broken."

"Oh, how kind you are!" said Mrs Johns. "Come and see Adam. He is in his playroom."

Peter was taken to see Adam. The big boy had a fine playroom with an electric railway running all round it.

It looked most exciting. Peter had a clockwork railway, but the electric one looked wonderful.

"Hallo!" said Adam. "Did you hear my leg was broken? No wonder it hurt me!"

Peter gave Adam what he had brought. The two boys talked hard. "You must come after tea and set my electric train going," said Adam.

"Well, I would," said Peter, "but I'd have to walk, you see, and I'd never have time to get here and back and do my homework too. I haven't got a bike like you."

"Haven't you?" said Mrs Johns. "Well – Adam is having a new, much bigger

119

bicycle for his birthday next week, and we were wondering what to do with his old one. Perhaps you would like to have it?"

"Good idea!" said Adam. "Then you can come and see me every day! Yes – you have it, Peter. I can't ride for some weeks, and by that time my new bike will have arrived. So I can give you my old one with pleasure. You were jolly kind to me and you deserve it!"

Peter was red with delight. "I shall have to ask my mother first," he said. "But I'm sure she'll say yes. Oh, I say – I have so badly wanted a bike, and now I've got one! I'll ride home on it and see what Mother says!"

Mother said yes, of course! "You've been a good boy and not grumbled because we couldn't give you a bicycle for your birthday," she said, "and now that your own kindness has brought you one, I am certainly not going to say no. You may have it, and Daddy and I will get the brake mended for you, and a new rubber for the pedal, and have it all re-painted. Then it will be as good as new!"

Well, you should see that old bicycle now! It looks just like a new one, and Peter keeps it so bright and shining. He is very proud of it and rides on it to school every day.

"Your accident brought me two things!" he said to Adam. "It brought me a bicycle – and a friend. Shan't we have fun together when your leg is better, Adam!"

Patter's Adventure

In a hole in a bank at the bottom of Mary's garden lived a mouse family. They were long-tailed field-mice, pretty little things, and as playful as could be.

Every day the mother mouse ran off to get food for the family. She knew exactly where to get it. Mary kept two doves in a cage, and she fed them each day, sometimes with grain and sometimes with bread.

The mouse was small enough to creep under the big cage where the doves lived and take a piece of bread. Before the doves could peck her she was out again, running down the garden with the bread. Then the little mouse family would have a lovely feast.

Now one day Patter, the youngest of the family, wanted an adventure. He had often heard his mother talk of the wonderful place where bread could always be found, and he wanted to see it for himself. So he followed his mother and saw where she went.

But as she came back she saw Patter. She dropped the bread at once and flew at him. "Patter! You bad, naughty little mouse! How dare you come out alone like this! Don't you know that Bubbles the cat is about?"

Patter had no idea what a cat was. He stared at his mother and his tiny nose went up and down. He curled his long tail round his little body and looked miserable.

123

"What's a cat?" he said.

"Oh, the baby! Fancy asking what a CAT is!" said his mother. "You'll know soon enough one day if you run about alone when you're no more than a few days old!"

She took Patter back and gave him such a talking-to that he didn't stir out of the nest for days. Then he suddenly felt that he must have an adventure again. And this time, he thought, he would go by himself right up to the doves' cage and find a bit of bread on his own. Then he could eat it all without having to share it with four brothers and sisters.

So off he went, a little tiny thing almost small enough to pop under a thimble!

Now Bubbles the cat had three growing kittens. They were five weeks old and very playful. They rolled about, they climbed out of their

basket, and they ran unsteadily over the kitchen floor. They often tried to catch their mother's tail.

"It is time you stopped being babies," said Bubbles one night. "You must learn what it is to hunt for mice. One day you will have to catch food for yourselves, and I must teach you."

"What are mice?" asked Ginger, who was the biggest kitten. Bubbles was astonished.

"What! You don't know what mice are! How ignorant you are! I will catch one and bring it in for you. You shall play with it, catch it for yourselves and eat it. Mice are very tasty."

So out Bubbles went, the same night that Patter was off on his adventure. She knew that mice went to the doves' cage, because she had smelt them. Perhaps there would be a nice, lively

125

mouse tonight. She would catch him and take him to her kittens!

Patter was running down the garden path to the cage. What a dear little mouse, with his woffly nose and long, thin tail and fine whiskers! The owl didn't see him or she would have pounced on him at once. The rat wasn't about that night or he would have had him for his dinner.

But Bubbles the cat was waiting by the cage. Patter didn't know that. He came to the cage and sniffed. He could smell CAT, but he didn't know what it was, so he wasn't afraid. He could smell bread, too, and that made his nose twitch more than ever.

Bubbles smelt him and sat there without moving even a paw. Patter ran nearer. He was just about to squeeze under the cage when he felt a strong paw pounce on him. He gave a loud squeak. "Eeeeee!"

He wriggled, but he couldn't get away. The paw held him, and he felt sharp claws sticking into him as soon

as he moved. He was terribly afraid. Was this CAT?

The paw moved and scraped him away from the cage. Then hot breath came over him and something sniffed him all over. Then, oh tails and whiskers, the mouth opened and Patter went inside! He was in the cat's mouth, surrounded by sharp teeth.

He squeaked again. He was not hurt, because Bubbles hadn't scratched or bitten him. No – she wanted to take him, whole and unhurt, to her three kittens to play with. They could chase him, pounce on him, throw him into

the air, and then eat him for their supper. She would teach them what Mouse was.

She padded to the kitchen window, still holding Patter in her hot mouth. His tail hung out from between her teeth. He squeaked and squeaked. Bubbles leapt up to the window-sill and dropped down into the kitchen. She purred, and her three kittens ran to her.

She dropped Patter on the floor, and he stared round at the wondering kittens. "There," said Bubbles. "That is a mouse. Sniff him well. All mice smell the same. Then chase him and see if you can catch him."

The kittens stared doubtfully at the

128

mouse. Then one put out a paw to him. Patter leapt away and ran into a corner. The kitten ran after him.

Somebody was sitting in the kitchen rocking-chair. It was being rocked to and fro, to and fro. Suddenly the rocking stopped, and a voice called out in horror: "My goodness! There's a mouse running round the kitchen! My goodness!"

Up got the person in the rocking-chair and rushed out of the kitchen. She went to find Mary.

"Can you come, quickly?" she panted. "You keep pet mice, don't you, so you're not afraid of them. There's a mouse in the kitchen! Bubbles brought it in for her kittens, but it's alive and running round. I can't bear it!"

Mary went into the kitchen. She put Bubbles outside and shut the door. The kittens were still staring at the mouse, not feeling very sure about it. Patter was not at all sure about the kittens either. He felt that he would like to play with them – but they were so big!

129

Mary saw him. "Oh, what a darling little field-mouse!" she said. "Go away, kittens, don't hurt it." She bent down to get it, but Patter, seeing such an enormous person suddenly bending over him, darted under a small table. Mary moved the table and put out her hand to catch Patter. He jumped away and ran right into the three kittens. Ginger put out a paw and tried to claw him. He didn't like that. He ran back under the table again.

And there Mary caught him gently in her hand. She closed her fingers round him so that only his little, woffly nose showed, and his tail hung out at the back.

"You're sweet!" she said. "I'll show you to Mummy. You're too little to be

out in the night by yourself. Whatever shall I do with you?"

She took the mouse to her mother. "Look," she said, "a baby field-mouse. Isn't he sweet? What shall I do with him? He'll be caught by Bubbles again, or an owl, if I set him free in the darkness outside."

"Well, dear, put him with your own pet mice," said her mother. "One of them died today, didn't he? Well, let this little thing take his place. He'll be quite happy with the others and much safer than running about by himself."

"Will he really?" said Mary. "I never thought of that! I'll put him into my mouse-cage now."

The mouse-cage was outside on the verandah. It was too smelly to be in the house. There were three mice there, a black, a brown, and a black-and-white. The little all-white one, Pippa, had died that morning. In the cage was a ladder for the mice to climb up and down, a dish of water and plenty of food. At the top of the cage

was a shut-in place, full of straw, which was the bedroom of the mice, very warm and cosy.

Mary lifted off the glass top, and slipped Patter inside. He was frightened now. He didn't like his adventure any more. He wanted to get back home to his mother and her nest. But he knew he would never, never find the way. Mary shone a torch into the cage and watched him.

He ran up the ladder and down. What an exciting place he had come to. But he couldn't get out of it. He sniffed here and he sniffed there – but there was no way out at all.

He could smell other mice. Where were they? He ran up a twig that was set there to lead to the bedroom and saw a round hole with straw sticking out. In a flash he was in the hole.

A ball of mice was curled up in a

132

corner. Patter nosed his way to it and it
dissolved into three surprised little pet
mice. They all sniffed at Patter.

"He's just a baby," said Frisky.

"Better make room for him," said
Whisky.

"Come along then," said Nipper, and
into the ball of mice crept Patter, happy
and pleased. He cuddled in, wrapped
his tail round everybody, stuck his nose
into his paws and went to sleep.

His mother was upset when he didn't
come back. "The cat's got him," she
said.

Bubbles felt sure her three kittens
had eaten him. "Did he taste nice?" she
asked.

The three kittens felt certain that the

133

mouse had escaped down a hole somewhere, but they didn't dare to tell their mother that. They knew they should have caught him – but they had been just a tiny bit afraid of the jumpity mouse. So they said nothing at all, but Ginger went and sat by a hole in the wall for a very long time.

Patter is still living with Frisky, Whisky and Nipper, and is as happy as the day is long. His nose is still woffly, his tail is longer than ever, and his whiskers are finer. Would you like to see him? He is a real live mouse and this is a real true story. He lives in a mouse-cage on my verandah, and we feed him every day.

"Eee!" he says and runs up his little wooden ladder to greet us. "Eeee!" Wouldn't you love a pet mouse like that?

The Train
that Broke in Half

Benny was a funny little boy.
He thought he couldn't do anything
well! He was always afraid of things, so
he was shy and timid, and hadn't any
friends.

"Benny, why don't *you* go in for the
races?" his mother said each summer
when the school sports came. But
Benny shook his head.

"No, I'm not good at running," he
said. "I'd only be last, and look silly,
mother."

"Benny, why don't you ask to belong
to the Cub Scouts?" said his father
when the spring came and the Scouts
and Cubs put on their uniforms and
went to have some fun in the fields.

"I'd be no good," said Benny. "I'd

never learn enough. You have to know a lot."

"Well, you could learn, as the others do," said his father. But no – Benny wouldn't try. He was afraid of looking silly and of being laughed at.

It was the same with everything. When he went to parties, Benny wouldn't play Musical Chairs because he felt sure he would be the first one out. At Christmas-time he wouldn't pull a cracker because he didn't like the bang.

"But, Benny, you've never pulled a cracker in your life, so how do you know you won't like the bang?" asked his mother. "You may love it, as the other children do. Don't be such a little coward."

Well, that was quite the wrong thing to say to shy Benny. He at once thought he *was* a little coward, so he became more ashamed and shy than ever. He thought that everyone must think him a coward, so he wouldn't play games in case he fell down and cried, and he

136

wouldn't go to any parties at all.

It was dreadful. His mother didn't know what to do with such a funny boy. The other children got tired of asking him to play with them and left him quite alone. So Benny played by himself all day long, and hardly opened his mouth at school. And yet, secretly, Benny longed to have friends and to shout and run and play. Poor Benny!

Now, not far from Benny's house ran a railway line, deep down in a cutting. Benny loved to watch the trains that ran by. He liked to hear them hooting as they raced past. He knew every one of them, and would have liked to wave to

the engine-driver, but he was much too
shy.

One day he was sitting on the fence,
watching the trains, when the long train
from the nearest big city came by. It was
a corridor train, so that the carriages
were closely joined together for people
to walk all up and down the train if they
wanted to. Benny liked that sort of
train, because he could see the people
sitting at the dining-tables and having
their dinner, and he could see people
standing in the corridors and looking
out of the window.

With a loud hoot the train came along,
deep down in the cutting. Benny looked
at his watch. The train was late, and it
was hurrying. Not more than ten
minutes behind it would come the next
train.

"You'd better hurry!" said Benny to the train. He wouldn't talk to other children, but he often talked to animals and trains and cars. The train hooted and went on.

And than a strange thing happened. The three last carriages of the train suddenly broke away and got left behind!

Benny stared as if he couldn't believe his eyes! The rest of the train went rushing on, and was soon out of sight. Just those three carriages were left behind. They ran a little way, and then stopped on the line.

"It's broken in half," said Benny to himself. "The train's broken in half!

Where's the guard? Will he pop his head out of the guard's van and see what's happened?"

But no guard popped his head out. He couldn't because he was in the other part of the train. He had gone to speak to the ticket-collector who happened to be on the train – so he didn't know anything about his van being left behind.

Nobody was in the last three carriages at all. They were quite empty. There they stood on the line, looking rather silly.

Benny soon saw that there was nobody in them. He stared and stared – and then had a dreadful thought.

What about the next train that would come rushing along in a few minutes' time? It wouldn't know those carriages were left on the line. Nobody knew but Benny. The signal-man didn't know. The engine-driver wouldn't know – and he would go crashing into them!

"Then there would be an accident," said Benny. "Oh dear! Whatever shall I do?"

For once Benny forgot that he thought himself a poor little coward, no good at anything. He only thought of the people in the train that was soon coming into that deep railway cutting, and would crash into the carriages there. Benny sprang down from the fence. "If I run for all I'm worth I could perhaps get to the signal-box in time, and tell the man to change the signal to red!" thought the little boy. "That would stop it!"

He began to run. Benny hadn't

141

thought he was any good at running at all – but how he ran now! His legs twinkled in and out, and his breath came in big pants. His chest felt as if it would burst, but Benny didn't care. No – he must, he must, he *must* get to that signal-box in time!

It was quite a long way – but at last Benny saw it in the distance. His legs were so tired that they could hardly run, but he made them go on and on until he reached the signal-box. The signal man was leaning out of his box, and he saw Benny.

Now in the ordinary way Benny wouldn't have dared to speak to a signal-man – but now he didn't care what he did. He could hear the train coming!

He turned his head, and there it was, rushing along the line – the train that would crash into the three carriages! Benny tried to shout, but his voice was so full of puffs and pants that he could hardly get his words out.

"Signal-man, change the signal to

red!" he panted. "There's some carriages left on the line – broken off the last train!"

The signal-man could hardly understand the breathless boy, but he at once pulled a heavy lever – and to Benny's great delight the signal that had been green for the train to pass by, changed to red – just as the train came rumbling up at a great speed.

The driver saw the signal change to red and he put on his brakes very

143

suddenly. With a long screech the train slowed down and then stopped. Passengers popped their heads out of the windows to see what was the matter.

Benny got back his breath. He yelled to the signal-man: "The last train broke in half! It left three carriages behind up the line. I only just got there in time to warn you."

"Good for you, young man!" said the signal-man. He ran down from his box and went to the engine-driver. Then the train went slowly on, taking the signal-man too, and soon everyone saw the

144

three left-behind carriages.

"That was a narrow escape," said the engine-driver, looking pale. "I'd have been right into those carriages if you hadn't put the signal against me."

"It's that boy who saved the train," said the signal-man, looking round for Benny. But Benny was gone! You won't believe it, but all his shyness and fear came back again when he saw so many passengers looking at him. He ran home quickly and went into his bedroom. He was trembling now. He couldn't think how he could have done such a thing!

That teatime his mother was full of

145

the whole affair. "Fancy, Benny," she said, "a boy saved the London train! He saw some carriages left behind on the line, and he tore to the signal-man to tell him – and the next train was saved. Oh, Benny – if only you could do a thing like that! How proud Daddy and I would be of you!"

Benny looked at his mother. He knew how often he had disappointed her because he had been so silly and shy and afraid. Now he had a big surprise in store for her!

"Would you really be proud of me?" he said. "I'd like that, mother!"

"Oh, Benny, I'd be so proud I'd run out and tell everyone about you!" said his mother. "But you're such a funny little quiet boy – you'd never do anything wonderful, you'd be too scared!"

Just then a knock came at the door – and who should be there but the signal-man! He knew Benny and knew where he lived – and he had come to say a few words to him. And behind him was a

146

crowd of children – the boys and girls of Benny's school, who had already heard about Benny from the signal-man!

"Where's Benny?" said the signal-man. "Ah, there you are! You're a hero, Benny! You saved the train! My goodness, I saw you running to my box, and I've never seen anyone run so fast in my life! Never! You'd win any race if you ran like that. I want to shake hands with you."

147

And he solemnly shook hands with Benny, whilst Benny's mother and father looked on in the greatest surprise.

"But was it our *Benny* who saved the train?" cried his father. "Good gracious! To think Benny could do that! Benny, Benny, I'm proud of you! I always thought you were a timid little fellow – but my word, you're a hero!"

His mother hugged him. His father clapped him on the back. The signal-man shook his hand up and down – and

in crowded all the boys and girls, yelling, "Benny, Benny! Tell us all about it. Come out, Benny, we want to see you."

And then, all of a sudden, Benny was a hero. He didn't feel a cowardly little fellow any more. He wasn't afraid of anything. He wanted to shout and run and climb. He was changed from top to toe!

"I didn't know I could do it – but I did!" he kept telling himself. "I was wrong about myself. I was silly and shy just because I thought myself to be silly and shy – but I'm not really. I'm brave and bold – I can run very fast. I can do great things! Oh, I'm glad, I'm glad! Everything will be different now!"

149

And so it is – for Benny himself is different, you see. The passengers of the train collected money to give to the boy who saved them, and they bought Benny a fine toy motor-car that he drives down the streets every day. And to hear him come hooting along at a fine pace, you'd never think he was once a poor, shy little fellow who couldn't say boo to a goose!

You never know what you can do until you try!

The
Lost Bus

Once when Miranda was going to school one day she missed the bus.

She saw it rumbling round the corner and she ran down the lane after it, crying bitterly. "Wait, wait! Wait, wait! Let me catch you. I shall miss school if I don't."

But the bus was gone. Miranda wasn't very old and she was very upset. She sat down on the grassy bank at the side of the lane and began to cry all over again.

"What's the matter?" said a voice, and a small man looked at her out of a rabbit-hole. "I've never heard anyone cry so much. What *can* be the matter? Can I help you?"

"No," said Miranda. "I've just lost my bus, that's all. You can't help me at all."

151

"Was it a nice bus?" asked the little man.

"Well – quite nice," said Miranda. "The usual kind."

"What colour?" asked the small man.

"Green and yellow," said Miranda, puzzled.

"How many wheels?" said the little fellow. "And did it have seats on the top as well as inside?"

"It had six wheels – and there are no seats on top," said Miranda, drying her eyes. "But what's the good of asking me all these questions? I tell you I've lost my bus and nothing you can do will bring it back. It's gone!"

"You wait!" said the tiny fellow. "My name is Tips and I've got a cousin called Tops. He's the guardian of all lost things. I may be able to get your bus for you."

He disappeared. Miranda was so surprised at all this that she didn't get up and go, but just sat there, wondering if the small man would come back.

He did come back. She heard a

curious clickety noise down the rabbit-hole, and looked into it. At first she could see nothing. Then she saw what looked like two little headlights.

"Parp-parp!" she heard, and up the rabbit-hole came a little green and yellow bus, tooting hard, driven by Tips! He was looking very pleased with himself. He drove right out of the hole and stopped the bus just beside Miranda. It was about the size of a toy bus.

He switched off the headlights. "It was so dark down the hole that I had to have the lamps on," he explained. "Well, here's the bus you lost. You said it had six wheels, but you made a mistake. It's only got four."

Miranda stared at the little bus and then at the proud little man.

"But I don't understand," she said. "Why have you brought me this dear little bus?"

"How stupid you are!" said the small man. "You said you had lost your bus, didn't you – a green and yellow one, with seats inside and not on top. Well, I went to my cousin, who takes charge of all lost things, and this was the only green and yellow bus that had been lost. So it must be yours!"

"But it *isn't*," said Miranda, and she began to laugh. "The bus I lost wasn't this one, really it wasn't. I lost the school bus."

"Lost the *school* bus!" said the little man, looking astonished. "But – how could you lose a great big thing like that? How very, very careless you are. I shouldn't have thought anyone would lose a great big bus like that."

"Oh dear. I don't mean I lost it like you lose money or a toy or something out of your pocket," explained Miranda.

154

"I was running to catch it to go to school – and it went without me. I was too late. I lost it."

"Oh," said the small man, looking very disappointed. "So that's what you meant. And you were crying your eyes out because of *that*! Well, well, perhaps I can help you after all."

He took a little tin from his pocket and rubbed himself with some yellow ointment out of it. At once he shot up as tall as Miranda. Then he rubbed the little bus.

155

"Gracious!" said Miranda. "The bus has grown enormous, too! I can even get into it!"

"Of course," said the small man – though he wasn't nearly as small now. "That's why I made it big. Get inside, little girl – and I'll drive you to school. It won't matter a bit if you've lost the other bus – you've got this one now!"

And will you believe it, he drove Miranda down the lane and out on the main road, and all the way to school at top speed! They actually caught up the school bus and passed it.

"Here you are," said the little fellow, stopping outside Miranda's school. "Out

you get. And don't lose any more buses! If you do, you know where to come for help! Goodbye!"

"Goodbye, Mr Tips," said Miranda, gratefully, and watched the funny bus speed away fast.

She went into school, feeling pleased and happy. What an adventure to have! She would go to that rabbit-hole the very next day and give Mr Tips a little present for being so kind.

But do you suppose she will know *which* rabbit-hole? There are so many there, you see, and she may not find the one that belongs to Mr Tips. I *do* hope she does, don't you?

The Five
Bad Boys

"Where are you going, you two?" asked Mother, as Donald and Jeanie went out of the door.

"Just to take some of the carrots we've grown to that dear little donkey in Farmer Straws' field," said Jeanie. "Look, Mother – aren't they fine carrots?"

"They are," said Mother, "and you're fine gardeners. All right, take the little donkey a feast. He's certainly a dear little thing."

"Mother, would he be very expensive to buy?" asked Donald. "You know how Jeanie and I have always wanted a pony of our own – and as we can't have that we wondered if a donkey would cost a lot of money."

"Yes, I'm afraid it would," said Mother. "And anyway we couldn't keep it in our tiny garden. You must just be content with going to see other people's horses and donkeys."

The two children went off with their carrots. The baby donkey was certainly adorable. He came running to the field gate as soon as he saw them, because he knew them very well.

"Hello, Long-Ears," said Donald, rubbing the grey velvety nose. "How are you this morning? Very hungry?"

The donkey's mother stood nearby, proud of her youngster. She never tried to come and eat his carrots. The children liked her too – she was so round and gentle and soft-eyed. She had often give the children rides.

A stone suddenly flicked against the little donkey's nose and it started back in alarm. "What's up, Long-Ears?" said Donald, surprised. Then another stone came flicking over the hedge and hit the donkey on the back. He ran off to his mother.

Donald and Jeanie looked round. "It's those boys again," said Donald, in disgust. "The Gang – Harry, John, Ronnie, Peter and Sam. They think themselves so grand and fine, going round making themselves a nuisance, ringing bells and running away, throwing stones and stealing fruit."

A squealing noise came to Jeanie's sharp ears. "What's that?" she said. "That squealing? It sounds like some

160

animal that's frightened."

They listened. Now Donald could hear it, too. He went out of the field and looked down the lane. The gang of boys were standing together, looking at something in the middle of the group.

"They've got a pup, I think," said Donald. "What are they going to do with it? They are such cruel boys that you never know what they'll do if they get an animal into their power."

Jeanie went pale. "Oh, Donald – don't say they've got a little pup and they're going to ill-treat it!" she cried. "You know how they stoned that poor duck the other day. They're horrible boys."

The boys *had* got a little pup. They were jabbing it with sticks, and it was

161

squealing. But when a car came by they hurriedly picked up the puppy and stuffed it into a sack so that it could not be seen.

"Did you see that?" said Jeanie. "They've put it into the sack. What are they going to do with it, Donald? Poor, poor little thing."

The gang of boys set off down the lane. Harry had the sack over his shoulder. John jabbed at it with his stick and grinned when a squeal came out of the sack.

The boys forced their way though a gap in the hedge and went over to a pond in the field beyond. Jeanie and Donald stood in the gap and watched them.

Ronnie undid the sack and out tumbled the poor little puppy. It crouched down on the ground, terrified and bewildered. Then Sam took it by the scruff of the neck and threw it right into the middle of the pond.

"Let's see how you swim!" he shouted, and all the boys laughed. Splash! The

puppy landed in the water and began
to try and swim at once, its short little
legs beating to and fro.

"Oh, Donald! Let's go and save it!"
said Jeanie, tears in her eyes. But
Donald held her back. He knew the
boys would turn on them and knock
them down, and he didn't want Jeanie
to be hurt.

"Now they're throwing stones at it to
stop it getting out of the water," said
Jeanie, beginning to sob. "Let me go,
Donald, I don't care what they do to
me. I'm going to help the puppy."

163

The puppy squealed in terror when the stones hit it as it struggled to get to the edge of the pond. Once it reached the edge, but John picked it up and threw it back into the middle again. It was getting weak now, and could hardly swim at all.

"It'll drown, it'll drown," wept Jeanie. "Oh, you are a coward, Donald, not to save it."

But Donald knew that far from saving the puppy he, too, would be thrown into the pond. He must save the puppy in another way. He was watching for two of his friends to come along. They were to meet him – then they would soon save that puppy!

"There they are!" he said suddenly, seeing Jim and George down the lane. "And Will's with them, too." He beckoned urgently, and the three boys came at a run.

"What's up?" said Will.

"That Gang again," said Donald. "They've got a pup, and they're stoning it in the pond. It's hurt and half-drowned, poor thing. Come on – let's go for those boys and get the pup."

The four boys, followed by Jeanie, ran into the field, yelling. The Gang looked round. Like all bullies, they were cowards, and when they saw how fierce and angry Donald and the others looked they were afraid.

"Come on, run!" shouted Ronnie, and the whole Gang took to their heels and fled. The puppy was left squealing and floundering in the pond. Donald ran to

the edge of the water. He and Will waded in and picked up the trembling little creature. It was bleeding from the stones, and was dripping wet and half dead with fright.

Donald tucked it into the warmth of his coat. Jeanie stroked its wet little head. The other three boys looked on in silence. They all loved animals and felt a fierce anger when they saw the tormented little puppy.

"It's such a dear little thing," said Jeanie, tears still running down her cheeks. "I think it must be one of Farmer Straws'. I know his collie had a lovely litter, and this little pup must have wandered away and been found by the boys."

A loud voice hailed them from the gap in the hedge. They looked round. Farmer Straws was there, looking very angry. "What are you doing in this field? Haven't I told you kids time and again not to trespass? Well, this time I'll take your names, and report you to the police."

"Sir, we went in to rescue this little pup," said Donald, showing the farmer the puppy cuddled in his coat. "Some boys were stoning it in the pond. Is it one of your collie pups, sir?"

"Yes – one was stolen yesterday," said the farmer. "Who's been stoning this poor little thing? And who's been stoning that young donkey, too? I saw stones flying over the hedge yesterday and hitting him, but when I went to see who it was, there was no one there."

"Same boys as stoned the pup, sir," said Jim. "We're going after them now.

We'll bring them to you sir, and you can deal with them."

"Good lads," said the farmer. "Stick up for the weak and those that can't help themselves, and you won't go far wrong. It's lads like you that can stop other boys from doing these things. Go and get those boys and bring them to me."

Jeanie went to the farmhouse with Mr Straws, to let the farmer's wife see to the puppy. On the way they passed the field where the little donkey was, and when he saw Jeanie he came running to the gate.

"I do love him," said Jeanie. "I suppose he isn't for sale, is he, Mr Straws? Donald and I would save up every penny if we could buy him."

"No. He's not for sale," said the farmer. "I'm giving him to my nephew as a present next week."

"He's very lucky, then," said Jeanie, and gave the little donkey one last pat.

Meanwhile, Donald, Jim, George and Will were hunting for the Gang.

"Better capture them one by one and take them to Mr Straws," said Donald. "We'd never hold them all at once. We'll get Harry first."

They got both Harry and Sam. The two were very frightened and tried to get away, but the four boys held them firmly, and took them off to Mr Straws, who promptly locked them into a shed, till the other three of the Gang were found. Before long Donald, George, Will and Jim had got all five.

Mr Straws unlocked the shed, and ordered the five trembling boys to stand up in front of him. Outside, to their horror, they saw the village policeman, tall and stern, with a big black notebook in his hand.

"Constable, these boys trespassed on my land this morning,"said Mr Straws. "They also stole a valuable collie pup of mine. They threw it into my pond and stoned it. I want you to take all five to the police station."

"No, no, no!" cried Ronnie, in terror. "My mum would cry her eyes out."

"Let us go!" begged Sam. "My dad would give me such a bad time if he knew we were taken to the police station."

"So would mine," said Harry. Peter and John were so frightened that they couldn't say a word.

"By rights I should throw you all into the middle of my pond and then throw stones at you," said the farmer. "You mean, cowardly, wretched little bullies! You wait till the news gets round, and see what people say about you! Constable, take them away."

"Don't take us to the police station – all the village kids will see us, and we'll never hear the last of it!"

"What you all want is a sound, hard smack," said Mr Straws. "Just so that you will know what pain feels like. You hurt that puppy – you hurt my ducks the other day – you stoned my donkey. You deserve to be well hurt yourselves, so that you may know what pain is. Constable, do you think these boys' fathers would punish them if I send them home instead of having them taken to the police station?"

The constable looked at the trembling boys. "I'll have a word with each father," he said, shutting his notebook. "We'll let the fathers choose. Either I take the boys to the police station and charge them, or their fathers punish them all and tell you about it, so that you know they're getting what they deserve."

"Right," said Mr Straws. "Find out straight away, Constable."

Well, you can guess what happened. Not one of the fathers wanted the policeman to take their boys to the police station, and, my word, what a hard slap each one got. They squealed as loudly as the poor little puppy had squealed when the stones hit it.

"It serves them right," said Donald to Jeanie that night. "They'll never throw stones again!"

He was right. They didn't. They were frightened and ashamed, and the Gang broke up at once. But that isn't quite the end of the story.

Farmer Straws sent to Jeanie and Donald and asked them to come and see him. They went, wondering what he wanted.

"It's about that little donkey," said Farmer Straws. "I'm not giving him to my nephew now. You see, he was one of those boys who stoned the pup – John Lewis. I'm not handing out any animals to him. I want the donkey to go to someone kind and decent – and so I'm giving him to you and Jeanie."

"Oh, sir!" said Donald, and Jeanie laughed aloud in joy.

"And mind you give your three friends a ride!" said Farmer Straws, with a twinkle. "The ones who helped to catch those five bad boys."

"We'll go and tell George, Will and Jim this very minute!" said Jeanie. "But there are five boys who will NEVER have a ride on Long-Ears the donkey!"

I know who *they* are, and so do you!

Somebody Saw!

It was Sports Day at the big Boys' School. All the Johns, Bills, Peters and Mikes were hoping to win a prize of some kind. How they practised their running and jumping and how they tried out the three-legged race for days beforehand! There were to be bicycle races too – quick ones and slow ones, and trick ones.

Most of the boys had bicycles, and they cleaned them up before the great day. George cleaned his up, too.

George's bicycle was very old. It wanted a coat of paint. Its pedals had very worn rubbers, and it was bent in several places.

"But it's a good old bike, all the same," George often said, when the other boys laughed at it. "I'm fond of it. It's taken me for miles and miles, and I've had jolly good times on it."

It *was* a good old bike, and George had never had a single accident on it. For one thing his father made him read the Highway Code till he almost knew it by heart – and for another thing he made George learn his manners.

Not only manners at home and at school – but manners on the road! "You

just remember that there are other people on the road, George," he said. "And don't forget that a spot of good manners can prevent an accident as often as keeping the Rules of the Road!"

So George waved on other bicyclists who wanted to pass him, instead of trying to out-race them, or swerving out at them as they passed. He stopped at the pedestrian crossings to let people walk over the road, instead of ringing his bell violently and making them jump. He put his hand out in good time before he turned a corner.

176

He was an excellent cyclist, and he had made up his mind to win one of the cycling prizes at the sports. If only he had a better bicycle!

"Harry's got one of the new racers," he thought as he cleaned his. "And John's just got a fine new one, as fast as any I've seen. And Patrick's bike is a beauty."

He cycled off to school, in good time for the Sports. The parents had been asked to come too. They all turned up, hoping that their boys would win prizes. It was a hot, sunny day, just right for School Sports.

George was no good at running. He wasn't much good at jumping either, and Patrick easily won the high jump. Harry won the long jump. Then came the three-legged race. George was tied to Jeffrey, who got a fit of giggles, and down they both went at once!

"Aren't you ever going to win something, George?" asked his mother, when he went over to her. "We've already had eight events, and you've been almost last in every one!"

"Wait till the cycling match," said George. "I'll win something there!"

But he didn't. He was a long way last

in the speed race. How could anyone hope to go as fast as Harry on his new racer, or Patrick on his red and gold bike?

He didn't even win the slow bicycle race, because someone bumped into him and made him fall off. He was fourth in the trick-cycling, which was riding without touching the handlebars at all.

"I would have been first if my bike hadn't been so old," he told his mother. "You see, it's not properly balanced now. I haven't won a thing! I'm sorry, Mother, because though I don't mind, I know you're disappointed!"

"I am rather," said his mother. "Your father was so good at sports when he was a boy."

The Sports came to an end. The prizes were given out and George looked admiringly at Harry's new cricket-bat and the grand football that John went up to get. The prizes were really very good indeed.

Then the boys went home. "Now be careful, because you're all going off together," said the Head.

"Don't act the goat – and remember, there are others on the road besides yourself!"

A lot of the boys did play the fool, of course. They always did. George couldn't help laughing when he saw Peter riding solemnly backwards down the road, instead of forwards, just as he had done in the trick cycling.

The boys didn't see a car following them slowly. They tore across the pedestrian crossing and made a woman with a pram scream, because she was already half-way across.

George stopped. "I say – don't be scared! Look, you've dropped your book." The woman was frightened and angry.

"You bad boys! Where are your manners, I'd like to know! I'll complain about you to your Headmaster!"

George rode on. Behind came the car, very slowly. It stopped when George had got off his bicycle. George caught up with the others, who were waiting for a traffic light to change. Two cars were there, too. The boys swerved their bicycles in front of the cars as soon as the lights changed preventing them from getting off quickly. One of the motorists hooted.

George waited, knowing that the cars would soon be well ahead of him. Then on he went again, and behind him came the car. He heard it and looked round. He swerved in to the kerb and waved it on courteously, and then waved on a man on a bicycle who seemed in a hurry.

The car stopped a little way in front. George saw two policeman in it. The driver beckoned to him. Oh dear – had he done anything wrong?

"Name and address?" he said to poor George. "And school, please?"

George gave them, his heart sinking. "What have I done, sir?" he said.

"Done?" said the police-driver, with a broad smile. "Well, you've just won the

Courtesy Prize for this town, that's all! We've been cruising round all day looking for someone on the roads who knows his Highway *Manners* as well as his Highway Rules – and you're the first person we've seen who knows them both."

"I *say!*" said George, astonished and delighted. "I've won a prize today, after all! I messed up everything I did at the Sports – and won a prize going home! What a bit of luck!"

The prize was a silver wrist-watch with his name on it – and it was presented by the police on the platform of George's school. The Head was delighted and how the boys clapped George!

"Good old George! He's won something for the school! We've got the Courtesy Prize because of George."

George, still has the watch and it's a beauty. I know, because I've seen it!

The Boy Whose Toys
Came Alive

There was once a boy called Sammy, who longed for his toys to come alive.

"I'm sure you come alive at night and have a lovely time!" Sammy said to them. "Well, why can't you come alive and really play with me in the daytime? Oh, I do wish you would!"

But they didn't – until something peculiar happened. It was like this. Sammy was walking along the lane to his home when a tiny rabbit flung itself out of the hedge and crouched down at Sammy's feet. After the rabbit came a fierce little weasel.

Sammy was frightened – but he picked up the little rabbit and held it safely in his arms. "You go away!" he said to the weasel. Just as he spoke a

184

small brownie came running from the hedge, smacked the weasel sharply on the back, and ran up to Sammy.

"Oh, you've saved my pet rabbit for me!" he cried. "Thank you a thousand times, Sammy! Snowball escaped this morning from her hutch, and I knew the weasel would be after her. Come here, you silly little Snowball!"

Snowball leapt from Sammy's arms into the brownie's. The little man petted and scolded her. Then he spoke to Sammy.

"I do feel so grateful to you for saving my pet rabbit. Is there anything I can do for you in return?"

Well, you can just guess what Sammy thought of at once! His toys!

"Yes, there is something you can do

for me," he said. "Make all my toys come alive! Can you do that?"

"Yes, I can," said the brownie. "But just tell me this first – are you a good boy or a naughty one?"

"Does that matter?" asked Sammy, going red. He was a naughty boy, not very kind to others, often disobedient, and so noisy that his mother was always having headaches.

"Well, it does matter a bit," said the brownie. "You see, your toys will behave like *you* when they come alive. It wouldn't do to have a nursery full of bad toys, you know. You'd get very tired of them. Also, you must promise not to tell anyone they are alive."

"Of course I promise!" said Sammy. Then he told a story. "I'm a good boy!" he said. "So do make my toys come alive!"

"Very well," said the brownie. He felt in his pocket and brought out a little tin. "Rub this yellow ointment on to your toys," he said. "It will make them all come alive."

186

Sammy was so excited that he forgot to say thank you. He tore off home with the tin and rushed up to his playroom. Which toy should he make come alive first?

"I'll make my clown come alive!" he said. So he rubbed a little of the ointment on to the clown's face. It acted like magic! The clown yawned, got up and ran round the nursery at once! Sammy could hardly believe his eyes. This was simply fine!

"Come here, clown," he said. "I want to have a look at you. Come and speak to me."

"Don't want to," said the clown, "I want to play with the bricks."

"Come here at once when I tell you!" said Sammy angrily. Do you know, that clown turned and made a very rude face at Sammy!

Sammy was so angry that he ran after him and slapped him hard. And that naughty little clown turned round and pinched Sammy in the leg! Then he ran off and got behind the toy-cupboard so that Sammy couldn't reach him.

"All right, you just wait!" said Sammy. He went to where he had left his tin of ointment and picked it up. He rubbed some on to his soldiers, his teddy-bear, his sailor-doll, his train, his horse-and-cart, his red ball, and his bricks!

Well, you should have seen the playroom after that! The soldiers at once began to march in splendid rows, and the soldier band began to beat the drum and blow the trumpets! It sounded beautiful.

The teddy-bear chased the sailor-doll, and the train shot round the playroom so fast that it bumped into the box of bricks. But the bricks were alive and sprang out of their box at once. They hopped about, and threw themselves here and there joyfully. One brick threw itself at the teddy-bear and hit him on the nose. The bear was angry and ran after all the bricks, which hopped about the floor like mad things, making a tremendous noise!

"Stop that noise!" said Sammy, who was afraid his mother would come in.

But do you suppose those bricks stopped? Not a bit of it! They danced about all the more, and two of them threw themselves at Sammy and hit him on the head!

Then the train got excited and ran over Sammy's foot. Its key caught his ankle and hurt him. Sammy held his foot and hopped about in pain.

"He thinks he's one of the bricks hopping about!" cried the sailor-doll rudely. "Just look at him!"

Sammy bent down and slapped the sailor-doll – and the doll gave a howl of rage, ran to the work-basket on the window-seat, took out a needle and pricked Sammy in the leg with it.

"Ow! Ow-ow!" yelled Sammy, hopping round again, first on one foot and then on the other. How his toys laughed!

Then the horse-and-cart began to gallop round the playroom – and you should have seen the horse kick up its little wooden legs! And how it neighed too! Sammy would have loved to listen if only it hadn't made quite such a noise!

"You do make a noise," he grumbled. "Oh, goodness me – now that ball's begun bouncing itself! I say, Don't bounce so high, Ball! Do you hear me? Don't bounce so high!"

The ball squeaked for joy and went on bouncing just as high as it wanted to. It bounced so high that it struck a vase of flowers – and over went the flowers, and down went the vase on to the floor, crash!

Well, all this noise was really too

191

much for Sammy's mother. She was resting downstairs, and she called up to Sammy, "Sammy! Come here! What was that you broke just now?"

Sammy went down to his mother, looking cross and worried. "I didn't break anything," he said. "The ball bounced up and knocked down the vase of flowers."

"Oh, Sammy, that was very naughty of you," said Mother.

"Mother! I didn't do it!" cried Sammy. "It was the ball, I tell you."

"Don't talk like that," said his mother. "And don't be silly. Balls don't bounce themselves."

But that was just what Sammy's ball *was* doing, wasn't it! Sammy went back upstairs, very cross and upset.

"Here he comes! Here he comes!" he

192

heard his toys say as he came in at the door. They were all waiting for him.

The ball bounced up into his face and hit his nose. The bricks, which had built themselves up into a high tower, made themselves fall all over him. The clown pinched his left leg and the teddy-bear pinched his right one. The sailor-doll pulled his laces undone. The train tried to run up his leg. The horse galloped his cart over Sammy's left foot and back again in a most annoying way, and all the soldiers ran at him and tried to poke through his socks with their guns and swords.

"What are you all doing, you bad toys?" cried Sammy.

The toys danced round in glee, shouting and squealing.

"You were never kind to us!" yelled

193

the bear. "We're having fun now you've made us come alive!"

And then the clown did a silly thing. He saw the tin of yellow ointment where Sammy had left it on the chair – and he ran to get it.

"I'm going to make the chairs and tables come alive!" he yelled. "Watch me, Toys!"

And then, to Sammy's horror, that naughty clown ran to the table and rubbed some yellow ointment on to its legs. Then he rubbed some on to the chairs and then smeared some on the cushions, the fender, the stool, the lamp and everything else he could think of!

"Stop, stop!" shouted Sammy. But it was too late – the whole of the playroom was alive!

Goodness, you never heard such a noise as that furniture made! The table at once began to dance round and round, first on one leg and then on the other. The chairs played "Catch" with one another, and banged all round the

room trying to grab each other with their legs.

The lamp tried to get out of their way and bumped into the stool, which was very angry and kicked the lamp so hard that it made a dent in it.

The fender began to laugh and stood itself up on end to see how tall it was. All the cushions rolled off the chairs, and tried to flop on top of the toys.

Sammy stood by the wall, looking quite frightened. It was like a bad dream. The armchair raced by and bumped into him. Sammy fell down at once, and all the other chairs raced over him. The fender laughed so much that it fell down with a crash.

"This is awful," said Sammy, trying

195

to get up out of the way of the stool, which seemed to think it would like to stand on Sammy's middle. The fender stood itself up again to see better. A large blue cushion flung itself on top of the surprised teddy-bear, and he sat down hard, with a growl. The fender laughed so much that it fell down again.

"*Silly* fender. Stupid fender!" said Sammy, feeling very angry with it. "Stop laughing!"

But the fender couldn't. Then the train began to laugh too – the engine, the carriages, and the rails – and they made such a noise skipping about and

squealing, that Sammy felt quite certain his mother would be angry enough with him to send him to bed for the rest of the day.

"Listen, Toys! Listen, everything," said Sammy, trying to make them stop. "I shall get into such trouble if you behave like this! I never knew such a noisy, disobedient nursery! Wherever in the world do you get these bad manners from?"

"You!" screamed everything. "We've learnt it all from watching *you*! That's why we're noisy! That's why we're rude and disobedient! That's why we're unkind! You taught us!"

The clock on the mantelpiece suddenly struck twenty-one without stopping and walked up and down like a policeman. The fender began to laugh again, and down it fell with a crash.

This time it fell on the clown, who was so hurt that he yelled the place down.

"Stop screaming like an express train!" cried Sammy angrily. "I know you'll bring my mother up here! Oh, how I wish I'd never made you come alive, you tiresome things!"

"Well, we *are* alive, so you'll have to put up with it!" said the teddy-bear rudely.

"If you talk to me like that I'll smack you!" shouted Sammy. He ran to smack the bear, and the fender stood itself up again to see the fun. But before Sammy could smack the teddy, the clown neatly tripped him up and down he went with a bang. The fender almost choked with laughing and fell down with a worse crash than usual.

Sammy kicked the fender. He kicked the stool. He kicked the engine and the red ball. He kicked everything he could reach, for he was in a terrible temper.

And then the toys and everything else decided that they would do a little kicking too. After all, if you are a table with four legs, you can do a lot of kicking! So they all rushed after Sammy, and the table got four fine kicks in all at once. Sammy gave a yell

198

and rushed out of the room.

"After him, after him!" shouted the table, and tried to get through the door. But it got mixed up with the fender, who was hopping along to see the fun, and it was a good half-minute before they got outside the door. Then the fender laughed so much that it fell down again, and the table jumped over it and left it there on the landing.

Now Sammy had rushed to his room and locked the door, but the nursery-things didn't know this. They thought he had run downstairs. So down they all went, helter-skelter, after him. Well, really, you never heard such a noise!

The table clattered down on all four legs, and the chairs jumped two stairs at a time. The coal scuttle rolled itself down and made a great noise. The stool hopped down, and the cushions rolled over and over. The fender stopped laughing, and slid itself down, bump-bump-bump, from stair to stair. It was enjoying itself thoroughly.

The clown and the rest of the toys

rushed down after the furniture. They all had to pass the open door of the room where Sammy's mother was trying to rest.

She saw the table gallop past, and she was most astonished. She thought she must be dreaming.

Then the chairs hopped by, and Sammy's mother sat up and stared. Then the lamp rolled by and the stool trotted along behind.

"I must be mad!" thought Sammy's mother. "Am I really seeing tables and chairs running along? Why are they running along? Where are they going? Oh dear, it really makes me feel ill!"

The fender came along and stared in at the room. When it saw Sammy's mother looking so frightened it began to laugh, and down it fell with such a

crash that Sammy's mother nearly leapt off the sofa. The fender picked itself up and hopped on after the others. Then the toys raced along too, and the engine clattered by with its carriages. The ball bounced along and the bricks hopped gaily. It was really an alarming sight.

Sammy was trembling in his bedroom. He heard everything racing by, and he wondered what his mother would say if they all went into her room – and then he heard them out in the garden! He went to his window and looked out.

"Where's he gone?" cried the clown.

"He must be down the lane!" growled the teddy-bear.

"After him!" shouted the lamp – and out of the garden gate they all went.

Well, they made such a noise that the brownie who lived in the lane peeped out to see what it was all about. And when he saw the live toys and furniture, he guessed at once what had happened.

"They must belong to Sammy – and he used his yellow ointment on them!" he cried. "Oh my, he must have been a bad boy to have such noisy, naughty toys! I shall have to do something about this!"

He ran into the lane and spoke to the toys and the furniture.

"What's all this? What's all this?

Please walk by me, one by one, slowly and without noise."

Everything was afraid when they heard the brownie's stern, rather magical voice. So one by one they went quietly by him – and quickly he dabbed each toy and each piece of furniture with a blue ointment.

When every one of them had gone by, the brownie called to them sternly. "In two minutes you will no longer be alive. You had better go quietly back to Sammy's playroom unless you want to be left out in the lane."

What a shock all the toys and the furniture got! They were so afraid of being left out of doors that they all turned round and rushed up the lane, through the gate, and into the house. And Sammy's mother saw them all again, rushing the *other* way this time!

"I'm dreaming again!" she said. "Oh dear, I must be ill or something. And here's that dreadful fender staring at me again, and laughing!"

Sure enough the fender began to

laugh, and it laughed so much that when it fell down with a crash at the bottom of the stairs, it couldn't get up again. And the two minutes were up before it could climb the stairs, so there it stayed, quite still.

But all the other things got safely into Sammy's playroom and just had time to arrange themselves in their places before the magic worked. They gave a sigh, and stayed as still as could be. There wasn't a growl from the teddy nor was there a creak from a chair!

When everything was quite quiet, Sammy unlocked his door and peeped out. He tiptoed to his room. He saw that everything was quite still. He wondered if he could possible have dreamt it all – but no, there was the little tin of yellow ointment still on the chair.

"Horrid stuff!" cried Sammy. He picked up the tin, put on the lid, and then threw the tin as far as ever he could out of the window!

"If my toys behave like me, then I must be a very bad boy!" thought Sammy to himself. "I'll try and be a bit better in future. Oh, goodness – here's Mother! I'm sure she will be cross with me."

Sammy was right – she was! She had made up her mind that Sammy must have thrown all the furniture and toys downstairs and then thrown them up again!

"What a bad, naughty boy you are, Sammy!" she said. "What do you mean by throwing everything downstairs? And do you know you've left the fender at the bottom of the stairs and I nearly fell over it! You will go straight to bed and stay there."

"Yes, Mother," said poor Sammy, trying to be good and obedient for once. He went to his room, but on the way he peeped down the stairs and saw the fender at the bottom.

"You can stay there!" said Sammy. "Laughing like that! I suppose you thought it was all very funny!"

The fender tried to laugh but it couldn't. Sammy went to bed, very sad and sorry.

And so far nobody has found that tin of ointment yet. But if you do (it's a very bright yellow), just be careful how you use it. You don't want to end up in bed like Sammy!

Colin is a
Good Policeman

Colin was saving up to buy a pair of skates. He had put all his Christmas money into his money-box and had put his Saturday money there too, and twenty pence that his daddy had given him for sweeping the snow away from the front path.

The money-box was a fat pig with a slit in its back. The money came out of its tummy, for there was a lock there, and when Colin put in the key and undid the lock, a little trap-door opened and the money fell out.

"Next week I shall be able to buy myself a pair of skates!" said Colin one morning, as he counted out his money. "Hurrah! Then I'll be able to go skating with Ned and Bill! That will be great!"

But something horrid happened before he bought his skates. A burglar came one night, broke into Colin's house, and took his money-box, Mummy's purse, Daddy's lovely field-glasses, some silver from the sideboard, and a beautiful cup that Daddy had won for a golf prize.

Mummy was dreadfully upset. The policeman came and took notes about everything. Daddy told him to be sure and catch the thief if he could, for Mummy had had a lot of money in her purse.

"And I had a lot in my money-box pig," said Colin, almost crying. "I saved

209

it up to buy some skates. Now my money is all gone. Please do catch the thief, Mr Policeman."

"I'll do my best," said the policeman, shutting his notebook. "Let me see where he got in, please."

The burglar had got in at a small window that led into the larder. The policeman made some more notes, and then went.

The thief was not caught, because the policeman had no idea who it could be. Day after day went by and still there was no news. Colin got more and more impatient.

"Mummy," he said, "won't that thief ever be caught? What about my money-pig? I wanted to buy my skates this week. Can't I get it back?"

"No, dear, not unless the burglar is caught," said Mummy. "And it doesn't seem to me as if he will be, now."

"But, Mummy, he simply *must* be caught, because I want the money for my skates," said Colin in despair.

"Well, dear, unless you catch him yourself, I don't see how you're going to get back your pig," said Mummy, laughing. "The policeman has done his best."

Colin went out into the garden, nearly crying. To think he had lost all his money like that, when he had saved up so hard. It was too bad.

Then he thought again of what Mummy had said – "Unless you catch him yourself, I don't see how you're going to get back your pig."

"If only I *could* find out who it was,"

thought Colin. "But I don't know how to begin. I don't know if the burglar was tall or short, fat or thin. I don't know anything about him at all." He thought hard for a minute, and then he frowned. "Wait a minute – I *do* know something about him! He must have been very small to get through that tiny window!"

He jumped up and went to the larder window. Certainly it was very tiny. Colin jumped up to the sill – and he noticed that as he jumped he left deep marks in the bed below. And there, beside his own marks, were two other marks, made by someone else!

He jumped down to look at them. They must have been made by the

burglar, for the ground was soft, and there had been no rain to wash out any marks since the robbery. They were deep, too, just as if the man had jumped up to the sill as Colin had done.

The little boy suddenly felt excited. He knew two things about the burglar now – he was small, because the window was very tiny, and he had big feet, because the marks outside in the bed were large. Good!

Colin found his mother's measuring tape and measured the footmarks carefully. Then he measured his father's slippers, and found that the footmarks

were even bigger than the slippers. The burglar had bigger feet than Daddy's!

"A small man with very big feet," said Colin to himself. "What else?"

He sat and thought – and then he rubbed his hands together, for he had thought of something else. Mummy had said how strange it was that Micky the dog hadn't barked at the burglar that night, for Micky always barked at strangers.

"Well, if Micky didn't bark, he must have known the man's voice and smell," said Colin to himself. "And if he knew the man, it means that the burglar must have come here often and spoken to Micky and given him tit-bits to make friends with him. I'm getting on! I'm looking for a small man with big feet, someone who comes here fairly often, and who Micky is friendly with."

Colin felt tremendously excited. He went to the window and jumped up to the sill again. He thought he would jump down into the larder and see how much noise he made. So down into the

214

larder he jumped – and as he did so his coat caught on a nail just below the window and tore.

"Bother!" said Colin, and looked angrily at the nail. And caught on that nail was a piece of brown cloth with a

215

little red line running through it!

"Gosh!" said Colin. "That's not a bit of *my* jacket! The burglar must have caught his jacket on that nail just as I did – and this is a bit of the jacket that he wore then! Oh, I *am* getting on! Yes, I really am. I know the burglar was a small man with big feet, who comes here often, is friendly with Micky, and wears a brown jacket that has a little red pattern running through it!"

The little boy rushed into the garden and thought of all the men who came to the house. Not the milkman – he was tall. Not the butcher – he had small feet. Not the dustman, nor the postman, nor the baker, because Micky wouldn't be friendly with any of them, and barked madly as soon as they appeared.

"What about the window-cleaner?" thought Colin. "No – he only comes once a month and, besides, he is fat. He could never get through into that tiny window."

There was the man who brought the eggs – but Micky hated him. There was the paper-man – it might be him. He was very friendly with Micky, and he was small too. Also he wore a brown jacket!

"I don't remember if he has big feet, though," thought Colin, jumping up, excited. "I must go and see."

The paper-man lived down the road. Colin did hope it wasn't him, because he was a nice man, and always ready for a joke. He was standing at the door of his shop as Colin ran up.

Yes, his jacket was brown, but it had a blue pattern running through it instead

of red – and his feet were not even as large as Colin's daddy's feet; so it couldn't be the paper-man. Colin was glad.

And then suddenly the little boy thought of the man who sometimes came to dig in the garden. He was a bad-tempered little fellow, and Mummy didn't like him. But Daddy said he needed help, and so he gave him a job in the garden whenever he could, and Mummy made him up parcels of bread and cake and fruit.

"We must always help others who are not so well off as we are," Mummy said to Colin, so the little boy had given Walters, the odd-job man, a whole

pound out of his own money at Christmas-time. He had emptied his money-pig and chosen the pound himself to give to Walters.

"Could it be Walters?" wondered Colin. "He is quite small enough to creep in at the window – and I know he has big feet because I heard him grumbling that he couldn't wear Daddy's boots, they were too small. Micky likes him because he throws him bits of his bread. But I simply *can't* remember the jacket he wears."

Now the very next day the odd-job man came again to dig the garden over. But as it was too frosty Daddy said he could chop wood instead. Colin went down the garden to tell him, and to the little boy's excitement he saw that Walters was wearing a brown jacket with a little red pattern in it – and at one side it was torn!

Colin's heart beat fast. So it *was* Walters who had been mean enough to steal from Daddy and Mummy, who had always been so kind to him!

219

The boy ran into the house as fast as he could and shouted for his father. "Daddy! I want you! I know who the burglar was last week! Oh, do get my money-pig from him and Mummy's purse and your golf-cup!"

220

"Colin! Whatever do you mean?" said Daddy, astonished.

"Listen, Daddy," said Colin. "I know all about the burglar. He's small, because he couldn't get in at the larder window if he were big. He has large feet, bigger than yours, because I measured his footmarks in the bed below the window. He's a friend of Micky's, because Micky didn't bark at him – and that means he comes here fairly often – and he wears a brown jacket made of cloth like this!"

He gave his daddy the bit of torn cloth. "I found it caught on the nail just below the larder window," he said. "And, Daddy, the burglar is Walters! He has got a coat on like that this morning, and it's torn!"

Daddy listened, getting more and more astonished. Mummy couldn't believe her ears.

"Why, you're a splendid policeman, Colin," she said.

"Oh, Daddy – I never did like Walters. You were always so kind to him, and

now see how he has returned your kindness! What are you going to do?"

"Ring up the police!" said Daddy, and he did. Well, Colin was quite right, for when the policeman went round to Walters' house, the first thing he saw on the mantelpiece was Colin's money-pig! And in a drawer was Mummy's purse,

quite empty, and Daddy's field-glasses. The golf-cup was in a cupboard, but the sideboard silver was gone. Walters had sold it.

Colin was so pleased to get back his pig – but, alas, it was empty! The thief had taken all the money out. Colin nearly wept with disappointment. "I shan't get my skates after all!" he said.

But he did. The policemen were glad to have found the burglar, for Walters had not only robbed Colin's daddy and mummy, but many others besides. And soon, no doubt, he would have taken things from other houses too. The police were glad to have found the thief, for they had been looking for him for a long

223

time – and what do you think they did? They sent to the toy-shop, and they bought a fine pair of skates for Colin!

The little boy opened the parcel, and saw the note with it: "A pair of skates for a good policeman!" and he squealed in delight.

"They are much finer than the ones I had saved up to buy. Oh, I *am* lucky!"

And you should just see him whizzing along on them! Goodness me, he goes as fast as the wind!

The Very
Fierce Carpenter

Mr Chip the carpenter had a very exciting workshop. He was always making or mending all kinds of things and the boys loved to go and look at his tools. He had so many – hammers, saws, screwdrivers, chisels – and it was marvellous to watch the way he used them.

But Mr Chip didn't like the boys. "Little pests!" he called them. "Miserable little mischiefs! Rude little monkeys!"

So, of course, although the boys like Mr Chip's shop they didn't like *him*. They made up a very silly game just to tease him. The game was to dart into his shop and pick up some shavings and the one who had the most was

their leader for the next week.

"It's a very silly game," said Jack's mother, when she heard of it. "And it will only make Mr Chip angry."

"But the shavings aren't worth anything to him, and it's fun to see who can get the most," said Jack. "He shouldn't be so cross and grumpy, Mother. He doesn't even like us to watch him when he's making something – and he's really very clever."

This silly game really made Mr Chip very cross indeed – so cross that one day he bought a dog! It was only a puppy at first, but it would soon grow. "And I'll teach him to fly at any boy who dares to come into my shop!" said Mr Chip, hammering away.

226

The boys would have liked the puppy – and the puppy would have liked the boys – but Mr Chip taught it to bark and fly at any boy who dared to dart into his shop to pick up a shaving. Soon the puppy could growl and show its teeth.

"One of these days that puppy will be a big dog, and will bite one of you," Jack's mother said. "It's too bad of Mr Chip to make it so fierce – I do wish you boys would stop teasing the carpenter. You make *him* fierce, too, and he's not really a bad fellow at all."

The puppy grew and grew. It adored Mr Chip, and Mr Chip thought it was the best dog in the world. He and the dog were always together, except when Mr Chip sent it for his paper in the afternoon.

227

"Now, Wags – off you go for my paper," he would say. And Wags would run out of the shop to the paper man at the corner, and bring back a paper in his mouth. The boys thought that was very clever of him. They were afraid of Wags now. He seemed as fierce as his master! It was quite dangerous to dart into the shop and pick up a shaving. Peter nearly got bitten!

"Horrible dog – and horrible master!" said Kevin. "I've a good mind to throw a stone at Wags when he goes to fetch the afternoon paper for Mr Chip."

"No, don't," said Jack. "That would be a hateful thing to do."

The boys found that the only safe time to dart into the shop and snatch up shavings from the floor was when Wags was out fetching the afternoon paper! But Mr Chip was ready for them! He caught Kevin by his collar and shook him until the boy was afraid his teeth would fall out.

He caught Ned and rubbed his nose in a pile of sawdust. He nearly caught Jack, and bellowed so loudly at him that Jack dropped the shavings he had snatched up!

"Little pest! Wait until I get you!" he roared. "I'll set my dog on you!"

Now Jack had a very big wooden engine, painted red. It wasn't big enough for him to get into the cab, which was a pity – but it was quite big enough to take with him when he went shopping for his mother, because it

229

could carry all the things he bought! He used to stuff them into the cab of his big red engine, and take them home like that.

The other boys thought it a wonderful engine. "Be better still if it had trucks," said Kevin. "We could all go shopping together then for our mothers, and use a truck each for our parcels. That would make shopping fun."

"Well, there's only room for *my*

shopping," said Jack, afraid that the boys might want to use his engine for all their parcels, too. It would be very heavy to pull then! "This kind of wooden engine doesn't have trucks!"

The mothers all smiled to see Jack go shopping, pulling his big engine along empty first of all – and then going back with the cab piled high with all kinds of things. It was wonderful what that engine carried! It even managed to bring home half a sack of potatoes once.

One afternoon Jack's mother called him. "Jack! Where are you? Oh, you're there, reading. I'm so sorry, dear, but I quite forgot to ask you to take your blazer to be cleaned when you went shopping this morning. It won't by back in time for the beginning of term if you don't take it today. Will you take it now for me?"

"Right, Mother," said Jack cheerfully. He really was a very good-tempered boy. He got up and went to fetch his engine.

"Oh, don't bother to take your engine, just to carry your *blazer!*" said his mother. "Surely you can take it over your arm, Jack!"

"My engine likes a run," said Jack. "It's just like a dog."

He pulled the big engine from its place in the hall cupboard, and stuffed the blazer into the cab. Then he hauled on the rope. "Come on," he said. "We'll hurry there and back, and then I can get on with my book."

But something happened on the way there. Mr Chip had sent his dog Wags out for his afternoon paper at just the same time that Jack was taking his blazer to the cleaner's. Wags had gone

232

to the man at the corner, dropped the money out of his mouth on to the pavement, and let the paperman stuff a folded paper between his teeth.

He turned to go back to Mr Chip, when a much bigger dog growled at him. Wags growled back. The dog flew at Wags, and Wags leapt sideways into the road.

There was a loud squeal of brakes, and a car swerved suddenly. But it didn't stop soon enough. It hit poor Wags on the back legs, and the dog crumpled up on the road with a howl. The paper fell from his mouth.

Jack was just nearby with his big engine, and he saw it all happen. The big dog ran off at once. The driver got

out of his car, and two or three children ran up. Wags tried to get up but he couldn't. His back legs were hurt.

"Who does this dog belong to? Does anyone know?" asked the driver.

"Yes. It belongs to Mr Chip, the carpenter," said Jack, coming up with his engine. "Oh, poor Wags! He's hurt! He can't get up."

"I'll go along in the car and tell Mr Chip to come and fetch his dog," said

234

the driver, and he got into the car again. He drove off. But alas, he didn't go to Mr Chip's. He drove straight past, and went on his way.

Jack waited and waited for Mr Chip to come, but he didn't. Wags dragged himself painfully to the pavement, picking up his master's paper in his mouth. Jack was very, very sorry for him.

"Wags! *I'll* take you to Mr Chip," said the boy at last. "The driver can't have told him. But how can I take you?"

Wags whined mournfully. Then Jack had a wonderful idea. He could pick Wags up gently, and put him on his blazer in the cab of the engine! Then he would pull the dog all the way to Mr Chip's shop.

"You won't be shaken too much because you'll be on my blazer," he told Wags. "I'm going to pick you up. I'll try not to hurt you. Don't bite me, will you, because I'm only trying to help you."

Luckily Wags wouldn't let go of the paper he held in his mouth, so although he growled a little with pain when Jack gently lifted him, he couldn't snap or bite.

Jack laid him on the blazer.

"Now you'll be all right," he said. "Soon be home, Wags!"

He dragged the engine slowly down the road, trying not to shake the hurt dog. Children followed him, and Wags growled again because he had been taught not to like boys and girls.

Soon Jack was at Mr Chip's shop. He left the engine outside and went in. Mr Chip was sawing and didn't see Jack at first. But when he caught sight of the boy out of the corner of his eye he pounced round on him at once.

236

"Ah! Got you this time!" he shouted.

"Mr Chip! Don't shake me! MR CHIP! WAGS HAS BEEN HURT!" yelled Jack.

Mr Chip stopped shaking him. "What's that? Wags hurt? Where is he?"

"He got knocked down by a car," said Jack. "I was there. He can't walk with his back legs. So I put him in the cab of my big wooden engine, on my old blazer, and brought him along. He's just outside. I couldn't bring the engine up the steps."

Quickly Mr Chip was outside. In a second he had Wags in his arms, and the dog dropped the newspaper and licked his master feebly. "I'm going to the vet!" said Mr Chip to Jack. "Keep the shop for me while I'm gone. My poor dog! He's badly hurt!"

Well! There was Jack left in charge of the carpenter's shop! What an extraordinary thing! He looked all round it. He felt the big heavy hammers. He admired the little stool the carpenter was making. He wished he could try out the big plane and the saw. What a lovely shop to have!

His friends came peeping in at him, amazed to see him there alone. He told

238

them what had happened.

"Ooooh! We could take every single shaving off the floor while Mr Chip's gone!" said Kevin at once.

"No. I'm in charge," said Jack. "That would be a silly thing to do. Anyway, he's dreadfully upset about Wags. We couldn't do silly or mean things when he's upset."

"Serve him right!" said Ned. "I'm glad that bad-tempered dog is hurt."

"Oh, no. You'd have been sorry if you'd seen him," said Jack. "Leave those nails alone, Kevin. You're not to take a single one."

"I wasn't going to," said Kevin. "I was just running them through my fingers. They feel nice."

"Here's Mr Chip," said Ned, suddenly, and all the boys ran away at once. Only Jack was left, standing in the shop. Mr Chip came in. He hadn't got Wags with him.

"Where's Wags?" said Jack at once.

"I've left him at the vet's," said Mr Chip. "Got to have something done to

239

his legs, poor fellow."

Jack was shocked to see tears in the carpenter's eyes. He must love Wags very, very much.

"Will he be all right?" asked Jack.

"Perhaps," said Mr Chip. "Don't know yet. I shall miss him badly. Thanks for bringing him back to me in that engine of yours."

Jack went home. He forgot about taking his blazer to the cleaner's, but when he told his mother what had happened she quite understood. People can't think of dirty blazers when dogs are hurt.

Every day Jack went to Mr Chip's shop and asked the same question. "Any news of Wags?"

And Mr Chip would tell him the latest news. "Not so good." Or perhaps,"He's better today." And then, "He may be back next week."

Once Mr Chip asked Jack to bring back his afternoon paper for him. Jack stuck it into the cab of his engine with his other shopping. Mr Chip stared at

the big engine and said what a fine
thing it was to bring back shopping in.
Jack agreed. He was still rather scared
of Mr Chip, but he rather liked talking
to him and watching him work. Mr
Chip didn't chase him away now.

"Wags is coming home tomorrow!"
said Mr Chip at last. He was smiling all
over his rather fierce face. "You might
come in and see him. He can walk all
right but he limps a bit still. Can you
come? He's got something for you."

Jack did go the next day, of course.
Wags was there, looking rather thin,

241

and limping quite a lot – but how his tail wagged when he saw Jack. He barked and then licked the boy all over on his knees and hands and face.

"Good to have him back again," said Mr Chip. "Now you come and see what he's got for you, Jack. Just a little present for someone who did him a good turn. A good turn to someone who's always yelled at you, and a good turn to a dog that's been taught to bark at you and chase you off! That's something worth doing."

He took Jack into his little sitting-room behind the shop. Jack stared in astonishment and delight – for there, beautifully made, were three fine trucks, one painted red, one green and one yellow!

242

"Trucks for that fine engine of yours that pulled my Wags home that day," said Mr Chip. "A present from Wags himself!"

"Oh, Mr *Chip!*" said Jack, and he flung his arms round Wags and hugged him. "Thank you, Wags, thank you. And thank *you,* Mr Chip. You made them for me. They're marvellous. Now all the children in my street can go shopping with me, and my engine can bring all the shopping home in its new trucks. I say! What will the boys say! You won't mind them using the trucks you've made, will you?"

"Not a bit," said Mr Chip, delighted to see Jack's excitement. "Come in any time you like, any of you, and watch me at work."

You should have seen Jack going home with his engine and three colourful trucks behind! All the boys came out to watch – what a wonderful sight! "Present from Wags and Mr Chip," said Jack proudly. "And Mr Chip says we can go in his shop any time we like. What do you think of *that?*"

And now Mr Chip often has his shop full of boys, and he doesn't mind a bit. As for Wags, he's as happy as can be to have so many new friends. He still limps, so you'll know him if you see him, by his limp and his crooked left hind leg. Give him a pat for me if you meet him!

On His
Way Home

"That's all for tonight," said the choir-master. "Richard, you sang better than ever. You've got more music in you than all the others here put together! I wish you could give them a little!"

Richard didn't even hear what the choir-master said. He was dreaming as usual, thinking out the tunes *he* could put to some of the carols they had been practising for Christmas week.

"Richard's dreaming of the time when he's grown-up and sings at concerts all over the world and makes more money than he'll know what to do with!" said one of the boys, who was jealous of Richard.

The choir-master looked at the dreamy Richard. He was certain that the

boy would become famous when he grew up. He lived for his music and his singing, and what was more, he worked hard at it too.

"Yes," he said, "Richard will be richer than any of us. He won't be able to help it. But let's hope he'll think of others besides himself when success and wealth come to him!"

Richard was the last to go home. He always was because he was slow and didn't think what he was doing. But at last he went out of the church, and looked up into the frosty sky, full of stars.

As he turned a corner, he heard the sound of a violin, and he stopped. It was a cheap violin – but how beautifully it was being played. The player spoilt it, though, by trying to sing to the melody.

Richard looked at him. He was an old and dirty fellow, with straggly grey hair, and stained, ragged clothes. His voice was hoarse and cracked as he tried to sing the lovely old carols. People laughed at him. Two boys sent a stone skimming down the road at him. No one threw money in the shabby hat put down at the man's feet.

"What a horrible noise!" said people passing by. "We would give him money to go away, but none for his dreadful singing!"

247

Richard was struck by the man's playing. A poor, cheap violin – but how marvellously played. He went up to the man.

"I like the way you play," he said. "You play wonderfully!"

The old man took his bow from the strings and peered at the boy. "I once had a famous name," he said. "I played all over Europe. Now I'm a poor old beggar-man scraping a cheap violin – and I can't earn anything for a meal, nothing for a bit of fire, or a warm coat. But it's done me good to have a boy come and tell me I can still play! Can you play too?"

"I can sing," said Richard. "I'll sing to your violin, if you like. Play the tunes of the old carols and I'll sing for you. Perhaps you'll get some money if I sing and you play."

The old man put his violin under his chin again. The first few notes of "Silent Night" came stealing on the night-air.

Richard lifted his head. "Silent night, Holy night," he sang, his voice as pure as an angel's.

The old man stared in amazement and delight – what a voice! Ah, this boy was a pleasure to play for. Violin and voice mingled, and people passing by stopped suddenly. Who was this singing? Who was it playing? Two masters of music, surely! But under the light of the lamp-post they saw only a young boy and an old and dirty beggar.

A little crowd gathered round, listening in silence. The choir-master came by on his way home, astonished by the voice, unable to believe it could be Richard's. The carol came to an end. A stream of coins poured into the hat. Richard looked down at the old hat in delight. What a lot of money!

The beggar ran his bow gently over the strings again. "Noel! Noel!" sang the strings, and Richard's voice joined in, clear and lovely to hear in the dark, frosty night.

The crowd joined in at the end of each verse, and once more the money rained down into the old hat. Then a policeman loomed up apologetically.

"Sorry – but you must move on," he said. The crowd sighed. What a pity! They had never heard carols they enjoyed more. Richard picked up the heavy hat and gave it to the old man.

"There must be enough here to buy you all you want this Christmas week!" he said. "I'm glad."

"Take half," said the beggar, but Richard pushed the hat away.

"No. I couldn't take money for singing to your lovely playing. You have it all." The boy ran home, humming a carol tune under his breath. The old man looked after him and the choirmaster heard him muttering to himself.

"Ah, you'll be a great musician one day, my boy – and you'll be a great man too! You won't only think of your music – you'll think of your fellow-men." And off went the old man with his pockets full of money – the first money that Richard had ever earned.

Good luck to you, Richard. You've begun the right way.

The Fly-Away Cottage

Joanna and Paul looked out of the nursery window. It was pouring with rain, and they had to go across the fields to fetch the eggs from the farm.

"What a nuisance!" said Paul. "It's such a long way down the road and over the hill to the farm when it's raining."

"Well, let's go the short cut through the woods," said Joanna. "We can put on our big rubber boots and our macs and sou'westers, and we shall be sheltered from the wind if we walk through the wood. It won't take us very long."

So they put on their rubber boots, and their mackintoshes and oilskin hats. They took the basket for the eggs,

252

called goodbye to their mother and set out. It *was* raining hard! There were big puddles everywhere, and the rain splashed into them and made them bigger still! The wind blew hard too, and altogether it was a very stormy, windy day.

Soon the two children came to the woods. They were glad to get among trees, for they were more sheltered then. They walked through the dripping trees, over the soaking grass. Then suddenly came such a gale blustering through the woods that the children were quite frightened.

"I hope the wind won't blow any trees down on us," said Joanna, looking round at the trees bent almost double in the gale. "I wish there was somewhere for us to shelter in just until this storm is over, Paul. Is there any cottage near that we could go to?"

"No," said Paul. "I've never seen any cottage here at all."

Just as he spoke, Joanna cried out in surprise and pointed to the left.

254

"Look, Paul! There's the funniest cottage I've ever seen. What are those things growing out of each side of it?"

It certainly was a strange cottage. Jutting out at each side of it were big feathery wings. They were perfectly still, and drooped a little in the rain. The cottage was very small, and had a yellow front door with one chimney that twisted here and there in the wind.

"It's the funniest cottage I've ever seen," said Paul. "I don't know whether to go to it or not. It looks odd to me. Goodness knows who might live there – a witch perhaps, or an enchanter. It's just the sort of cottage

255

you see in a book."

The two children stood looking at it, and the rain fell more and more heavily on them.

"It's raining cats and dogs," said Paul, and, my goodness me, just as he said that, his words came true. It really *did* begin to rain cats and dogs! A large black kitten fell on Joanna's head, and a little white dog fell down by Paul. Then two tabby cats tumbled near Joanna and three collies around Paul. The children stood looking at them in amazement. Then they looked up at the sky. It was full of cats and dogs, all

256

falling to earth like rain!

"Quick! Run to the cottage!" said Paul, in a fright. "We don't want hundreds of dogs and cats on our heads! It must be a very bad storm if it rains cats and dogs!"

So they ran through the falling cats and dogs to the funny little cottage. Joanna thought she saw its wings move a little as they came near. A black cat fell on to her shoulder and made her squeal. She rushed to the cottage door and turned the handle. She and Paul ran inside and slammed the door behind them.

A smell of new-made cakes was in the cottage. The children gazed around the room they were in. A small woman

with green wings growing out of her shoulders looked round at them from the fireplace.

"Now then, now then, what do you mean by rushing in like that without so much as a knock at the door or a ring?" she said grumpily. "Here I've got my oven door open and my cakes are baking as well, and you come in and make a draught like that. It's enough to make them all go flat, so it is."

The children were so surprised to see such a funny person that they couldn't speak. The little woman was fat and round and she wore a sort of sun-bonnet on her head. Her cheeks were hot from the fire, and she shut her

258

oven door with a slam.

"Well?" she said. "Haven't you a tongue in your heads, either of you? What do you want? Have you come to buy any of my cakes?"

"No," said Paul. "We didn't know you sold them. Are you a fairy?"

"I'm a pixie woman," said the funny little person, taking off her spectacles and polishing them on her big white apron. "I'm the famous Mother Mickle-Muckle, whose cakes are bought for all the best parties in Fairyland and Witchland. Haven't you ever heard of me?"

"No," said Joanna, feeling rather excited to see a real pixie person. "I'm so sorry if our opening the door has spoilt your cakes. But, you see, it's raining cats and dogs outside and we had to run for shelter."

"Cats and dogs!" said the pixie woman in surprise. "Nonsense!"

Just as she spoke a large brown and white dog fell down the chimney into the fire. It jumped out at once and ran

259

barking round the kitchen. Mother Mickle-Muckle picked up a frying-pan and ran after it.

"Get out, you clumsy creature!" she said. "I won't have animals in my nice clean kitchen!"

She opened the door and the dog ran out into the wood. But no sooner had the pixie woman shut it than two big cats fell down her chimney, and when they had jumped out on the hearthrug they began to fight, spitting and snarling at one another in a spiteful manner. The pixie picked up a rolling-pin and rushed angrily at the cats.

They flew at her and scratched her on the hand. Then out of the window they jumped, still hissing at one another.

"Look at that now!" said Mother

Mickle-Muckle, showing her hand to the children. "I won't stay here a minute longer! I hate dogs and cats falling down my chimney! Cottage, fly to Topsy-Turvy Land!"

Before the children could say a word the cottage spread its two feathery wings and flew up into the air! Yes, it really did! Joanna rushed to a window and she saw its wings beating the air like a bird's, and, as she watched, the trees were left behind and the cottage rose high into the air.

"Ooh!" cried Joanna in the greatest astonishment. "The cottage is flying away!"

"Of course," said the pixie, busy rolling out some pastry on the kitchen table. "It's Fly-Away Cottage, didn't you know that? It's famous all over the world."

261

"Well, *I've* never heard of it," said Joanna. "Have you, Paul?"

"Never," said Paul, looking in wonder out of the window, gazing at fields and woods below them.

"Then you are two silly, ignorant children," said Mother Mickle-Muckle quite crossly. "I don't know where you go to school, if they don't teach you things like that."

"I wish we *were* taught things like that!" said Joanna. "It would be much more exciting to learn about this Fly-Away Cottage, and you, than about bays and rivers."

Mother Mickle-Muckle was pleased. She took a plate of chocolate buns from the cupboard and put them down in front of the children.

"You can each have two," she said.

"We shan't arrive at Topsy-Turvy Land for another hour or two. Take off your coats and hats and sit down."

"Whatever will Mother say if we don't go back to dinner?" said Paul. "I don't think we ought to go to Topsy-Turvy land, Mother Mickle-Muckle, though I'd love to."

"You'll *have* to go," said the pixie, popping another tin of cakes into the oven. "I am taking some cakes to the Big Little Goblin for his party this afternoon and he would turn me into a biscuit or an ice-cream if I were late."

"Big Little Goblin!" said Joanna in surprise. "Nobody can be big and little, too."

"Oh, can't they?" said Mother Mickle-Muckle, rolling out some more dough. "Well, let me tell you, my clever little girl, that the Big Little Goblin is little in height but very big in width. That is, he is very short and very fat, and he is the King of Topsy-Turvy Land because he is the stupidest person there."

"Then why do they make him King?" asked Paul, astonished.

"Oh, everything is upside-down in Topsy-Turvy Land," said the pixie. "The stupidest is King and the cleverest is a beggar. Now just sit down and keep quiet whilst I decorate these cakes. We'll be passing over the sea in a little while, and you can watch the ships."

It was strange to be in a little cottage flying high above the clouds. The two children looked out of the windows and saw the ships on the sea, and then at last they were over land again. The cottage swooped down and landed with a bump on a little hill. The children were thrown off their feet, but Mother Mickle-Muckle didn't seem to mind.

She put some cakes into a basket and opened the door. "Come along," she said.

The children followed her – and how surprised they were to see the land they had come to. Everything was Topsy-Turvy!

The houses stood on their chimneys, and the people had to have ladders to get up to their front doors. It was really most peculiar. The people walked the right way up but they all wore a large boot or shoe on their heads instead of a hat. Joanna and Paul wanted to laugh whenever they met anyone.

The people were mostly small and fat, and they all had funny little button noses and pointed ears. They wore their coats back to front and they talked very loudly in high voices.

The Big Little Goblin lived in a small cottage and didn't look a bit like a king. He wore a red button-boot on his head, and round one of his legs was a golden crown. He took the basket of cakes from Mother Mickle-Muckle and peered at them to see if they were all right.

"He's a funny sort of king," said Joanna, when they came out of the cottage. "I should have thought he would have lived in that big palace over there." She pointed to a high, shining palace a little way off.

"Oh, that's where the cleverest man lives, the beggar I told you of," said the pixie woman. "This is Topsy-Turvy Land, remember. Beggars live in palaces and kings live in cottages."

Joanna stopped to watch a Topsy-Turvy Man walk up the ladder to his upside-down front door. She thought it must be very funny to walk on ceilings and see your fire burning upside-down.

"Come along, come along," said Mother Mickle-Muckle impatiently. "I

266

must get to Giant Too-Tall's before one o'clock with a jam roll."

They hurried back to where the Fly-Away Cottage was waiting for them. It was waving its feathery wings in the air, and was so anxious to be away that it rose up in the air almost before Joanna had gone through the door. She nearly fell out as it rose with a jerk and Paul just caught her in time and pulled her into the kitchen.

"We'd better have our dinner whilst the cottage is flying to Giant Too-Tall's," said the pixie woman, and she set the table with a white cloth. For their dinner she gave them hot ginger buns, cherry pie and cheese biscuits straight from the oven. They liked it very much. The cottage flew steadily through the air whilst they ate, and when next the children looked out of the window they saw a big black cloud in front of them with something glittering in the middle of it.

"There's a castle right in the middle of the cloud!" said Joanna in surprise. "Goodness, how wonderful!"

Sure enough, there was! The cottage flew into the thick cloud and set itself down in the castle yard. The pixie woman took a small jam roll out of the oven.

"Is that for a giant?" asked Paul, laughing. "Goodness, he must be a small giant!"

"You wait and see!" said Mother Mickle-Muckle, and she opened the

268

door of her cottage.

"Coo-ee!" she called, in a high, bird-like voice. "Coo-ee!"

The door of the great castle opened and out came an enormously tall giant with eyes as big as a dinner-plate. Joanna and Paul felt quite frightened

and ran back into the cottage.

"Have you brought my jam roll?" called a thundering voice and the cottage shook from top to bottom.

"Yes, come and get it," answered the pixie woman and she held out the jam roll she had made. The children saw a big hand come down to get it and dear me, what a very peculiar thing happened! As soon as the jam roll touched the giant's hand, it grew ten times as large, and was the biggest jam roll the children had ever seen in their lives!

"Thanks," said the giant's booming voice, and he gave the pixie woman a coin as large as a saucer. But as soon as it touched her hand it became small, and she slipped it in her pocket.

"Have you got visitors in your Fly-Away Cottage?" suddenly asked the giant and he bent down and looked through one of the windows. "Ho, children! Come along with me and play with my daughter!"

"Good gracious me, no!" cried the

pixie woman. "She would think they were dolls and would break them in a second."

"You give them to *me*!" said the giant and he tried to open the window to get at the children. But the pixie woman slapped his hand smartly with her rolling-pin so that he cried out in pain, and she called out: "Fly away, cottage, to the cave of the dwarf!"

271

The cottage at once spread its wings and left the black cloud with its great castle towering in the midst. It flew into the blue sky, and the two children were delighted to leave the tall giant behind.

The cottage flew lazily along, and the pixie woman looked at the clock. It said three o'clock. She tapped sharply on the wall of the cottage and cried: "Now then, Fly-Away Cottage, hurry up or we shan't be at the dwarf's cave in time for tea. He must have his cherry buns for it's his birthday party."

The cottage began to flap its wings so fast that it jerked about and the children sat down suddenly on the floor. Cups flew off the dresser and a chair fell on to the pixie woman's toe

272

so that she cried out in pain.

"Now, now," she shouted, banging the cottage wall with her rolling-pin, "what are you thinking of, cottage, to fly so fast? Be sensible. We don't want to be jerked out of the windows." They were passing over the sea again, but it was a very odd sea, for it was bright yellow, streaked with pink.

Time went on and soon the hands of the clock pointed to four. A mountain came in sight, standing right up in the middle of the yellow sea, just like a pointed island. The cottage flew to it and perched on the very top. The children wondered if it would slide down – and no sooner did they wonder it than the cottage *did* slide down! What a funny feeling it was – just like going down in a very swift lift!

Bump! The cottage reached the bottom and the children fell over again. When they picked themselves up they saw the pixie woman going out of the door with a basket of cherry buns.

273

"Don't come with me," she said. "The Tick-Tock Dwarf is bad-tempered and might want to keep you for servants. Stay here."

So the children stayed where they were, and peeped out of the door. Joanna saw a strange-looking flower growing not far off and ran out to get it. As she stooped to pick it she heard a voice say: "Ha! Here are some children! Let's take them prisoners!"

She looked up and saw a tiny dwarf staring at her, and not far away were about a dozen others like him. They all had long beards reaching to the ground, and wore long-pointed shoes on their big feet. Joanna was frightened and she ran back to the cottage and slammed the door, hoping that the pixie woman would return very soon.

But she didn't come. The dwarfs surrounded the cottage and came closer and closer. Paul locked the door and fastened all the windows.

"I believe there's a dwarf coming

274

down the chimney!" he said suddenly, and sure enough, there was!

"They'll capture us!" said Joanna, looking ready to cry. Paul peeped out of the window to see if the pixie woman was coming but there was no sign of her.

So in despair he cried out to the cottage: "Fly-Away Cottage, please fly

275

away from here and take us home!"

At once, the cottage spread its wings and rose into the air! The children were so glad. The dwarf who was climbing down the chimney got out again in a great hurry and jumped to the ground just in time. The cottage flew over the yellow and pink sea at a great pace. Joanna and Paul were glad to leave the dwarfs' island but they were worried about the pixie woman. What would she do? Would she have to live on the island all her life?

Suddenly they heard a cross voice

276

shouting. They looked out of the window. Behind them flew the pixie woman trying her hardest to keep up with the cottage.

"Open the door and let me in!" she shouted. "You stupid, silly children, open the door."

They opened the door, and Mother Mickle-Muckle flew in. She sat down by the fire and panted. She was very cross with them.

"Flying off with my cottage like that!" she said. "I never heard of such a thing! I shall take you both straight back home. I really don't know what you'll do next!"

The children were *so* glad to be flying home. They had had quite enough adventures for one day. Just as the

277

clock hands pointed to twenty past four the cottage flew downwards, and the children saw that they were in their very own garden! How glad they were! It had stopped raining, and the sun was shining. They took up their mackintoshes and hats and stepped out of the strange Fly-Away Cottage.

"Good-bye, Mother Mickle-Muckle," they said. "Thank you for our nice dinner and all the adventures."

"You're welcome to them," said the little pixie woman, putting another tin of cakes into her oven and slamming the door. "Come and see me again when it's raining cats and dogs!"

Off they ran and the last they saw of the Fly-Away Cottage was a speck in the air that looked like a kite as the cottage flapped away to the west where the sun was sinking slowly. "I *do* hope we see it again if ever it rains cats and dogs," said Joanna. I'd like to, too, wouldn't you?

Adventure
in the Afternoon

Ian had a camera. He had had it for his birthday, and he was very pleased with it indeed. It wasn't a new one – it was a very old one, really, that his father had seen in a shop and had bought second-hand.

"New cameras are much too expensive," he told Ian. "And, anyway, it is best to learn on an old one – and this is quite a good one. Here's a little instruction book to go with it – it tells you exactly what to do when you want to take a picture."

Ian was thrilled! A camera! Aha – now he could take his own pictures – and what beauties he would get.

"What are you going to photograph?" said Lisa, his sister. "Will you take me,

279

Ian? Id like you to take a snap of me."

"Oh *no,*" said Ian. "I'm not going to waste my precious films on snapshots of *people,* Lisa. Anybody can do that."

"Well, what are you going to photograph?" said Lisa. "Birds? Animals?"

"No," said Ian. "They won't keep still enough for me. I'm going to take pictures of cars and trains and aeroplanes. I'm going to make my own book of cars, to begin with. I shall photograph every kind of car! It will be great fun watching out for them and photographing them."

"Yes. That should be good fun," said Lisa. "Are you going to take a picture of our car, Ian? If you do, I could sit at the wheel as if I'm driving it. Do let me."

So Ian took his first picture – and it was of his father's own car, a Ford, with Lisa sitting up at the wheel as if she were driving it!

He wandered off, with his camera on a strap round his neck. He felt grand with a camera of his own. But he didn't mean

280

to take the things people usually took. No – he was going to take pictures of the things he was most interested in, and those were cars, planes and trains. Ships, too, when he was by the sea.

For the next week Ian had a fine time. He took a picture of a beautiful Rolls Royce, complete with a very grand chauffeur. He took a picture of a tiny little baby-car with a dog at the back. It had been left there to guard the car, and it barked loudly and fiercely at Ian when he came up with his camera.

"Don't you want your picture taken?" said Ian, and he clicked the camera.

"Well – I've taken it! And if you come out on it with your mouth wide open, barking madly, don't blame *me.*"

When he had finished the whole film his father showed him how to develop each picture. Soon Ian had twelve beautiful pictures of cars to stick into his Car Book. He was very proud and pleased.

"You've really done well with your first film," said his father in surprise.

"Well, I read that little book of instructions carefully first," said Ian, "and did exactly what it said."

"Sensible of you," said his father. "Most people rush at a new thing – they don't trouble to learn anything about it first, and then they wonder why they get poor results. You deserve your camera, Ian."

Ian went on with his photographing of all kinds of cars. He got Ford Fiestas and Volvos, and Volkswagens and Metros and Rovers and Vauxhalls – in fact, all the cars you see rushing about on the roads each day. I expect you know as many as he did.

He stuck the pictures of them in his

283

book. "I've got nearly every make of car now," he told his father. "I've got American cars too – and look, that's a French one – and there's another. I haven't got an Italian one yet. There's room for that, if only I can get one. They're lovely cars, aren't they, the Italian ones?"

His father didn't know as much about cars as Ian did, and he laughed. "Funny hobby, this, of yours," he said to Ian. "I don't know that it's much use, really;

it's fun for you, of course, but, honestly, your book looks rather like a catalogue of second-hand cars."

Ian didn't mind. He enjoyed his hobby, and he loved taking his camera out, ready to snap any new or unusual car that he saw. It was fun to snap them and even more fun to develop the film and see what kind of picture he had got.

One afternoon he was sitting by the roadside, waiting for cars to come by. There was a lovely view to be seen from the place he had chosen and cars often pulled up to look at it. Then Ian could snap them if they were cars he wanted.

It was very hot indeed. Ian moved out of the sun and snuggled into the greenery of the hedge. His eyes shut. He was asleep!

He was awakened by the sound of a car pulling up near to him. He opened his eyes, yawned and poked his head out of the shady greenery around. Then he sat up straight in delight.

An Italian car! A real beauty – a big yellow one with bright silver lines

285

shining here and there. What a car! Just what he wanted for his book of car photographs.

He pulled his camera case over to him and took out his camera. He saw a man get out of the car and walk to the wall on the other side of the road. He had something in his hand, but Ian couldn't see what it was.

To the boy's surprise the man lifted his hand and threw what he was holding over the wall. Then he walked back to the car. "They'll be off again in half a jiffy," thought Ian. "I must snap the car at once or I'll miss it. What a beauty! I might never see such a fine Italian car again!"

286

He hurriedly knelt up on one knee and squinted down at the little camera mirror that told him whether the car was in his picture or not. It was – right in the middle, shining beautifully in the sun. The man was just walking over to it.

Click! Ian snapped down the little lever that took the picture, and at the same moment the driver revved up his engine – *rrrrrr-rrrrrr-rrrr!*

The car shot off at top speed. Nobody had spotted Ian in the shade of the hedge. Nobody had heard the click of his camera. How Ian hoped that his picture

287

would come out well! What a beautiful car to add to the collection in his Car Book!

He was walking home, longing to develop his roll of film and see what the picture of the Italian car was like, when he saw a white car coming along in the distance. Ian saw a sign glowing on it:

POLICE

"A police car," he said to himself. "A Sierra, and jolly fast too, I should think. I wish they'd stop, because I've got just one more picture to take on this film – and although I've got plenty of Sierras, I've never had one yet with POLICE showing on it."

Just as if the car had heard his wish it slowed down and stopped beside him! Ian hurriedly took his camera out of his case. Now – he could snap this police car.

But before he could snap the car, a uniformed policeman put his head out of the window. "Hey, Sonny! Seen any cars along here lately?"

"Only one in the last half-hour," said

Ian. "I fell asleep in the hedge."

The policeman gave an exclamation of annoyance. "Well, you won't be much help then. What was the car you saw?"

"An Italian car," said Jack. "It stopped just by me, and the noise of the engine woke me up."

"Ha! Good!" said the policeman. "Then you can tell me who was in the car – how many – and what they were like."

"Oh – no – I can't tell you that," said Ian, trying to think hard. "I didn't notice. I just saw a man get out of the car and throw something over the wall down there – some rubbish, I suppose – and then he got back and the car drove away at once."

"What was the man like?" asked the policeman at once.

"I don't know," said Ian. "I really didn't notice, sir."

"Think of that!" said the policeman in an exasperated voice, turning to another man in the car. "Here's a boy who had a good chance of seeing how many there were in the car, what they were like, and everything – and all he knows is what the car looked like!"

Ian felt hurt at the man's tone. "Well,

290

sir, I know you think I'm jolly stupid," he said. "But actually I was photographing the car for my Car Book – so naturally I didn't bother about the people in it."

Then things happened very quickly!

The three policemen in the car exclaimed loudly, one of them hauled Ian into the car, and another whipped his camera case off his shoulder!

"He may have got just what we want!" said one of them. "We'll get the snap developed immediately! Johns, you drop off at the wall where this youngster says he saw one of the men throw something over, and see what you can find. We'll drive on to the police station and get this film developed at once."

"But it's *my* film!" began Ian indignantly. "I always develop my own films. What's all the excitement about?"

"Well, you deserve to know, seeing that it is likely you may be going to present us with a photograph of one or two people who are concerned in a robbery of valuable State papers," said the first policeman. "We've an idea who they are, but we've no proof at the moment. All we know is that they drove off in a big Italian car."

Now it was Ian's turn to get excited! Fancy his camera snapping the very car with the robbers in – and maybe the very robbers themselves. Ian

remembered the man who had been walking towards the car just when he had snapped it. Surely he would be in the picture?

One of the policemen dropped off at the wall and jumped over it to see what he could find. He hoped to get the case in which the stolen papers had been kept. It would be empty, of course – but there might be fingerprints on it.

The police car sped on to the big police station in the next town. The film was taken from Ian's camera and was soon being developed in a little darkroom. Ian watched in excitement.

At last one of the policemen gave a whistle and held up the roll of film to the light. "Look here! This is the car –

293

and who's that beside it? It's Lennie Richardson, isn't it? We thought he was in on this. And look, here's a man at the wheel, he's come out plainly – my word, it's Pete Lucien!"

"Is it a good snap?" asked Ian, patiently trying to get a peep of it.

"Fine! Couldn't be better!" said the policeman. "What a bit of luck for us! Got the car *and* the men all in one picture – absolutely positive proof of the thieves concerned. Sonny, you did much better than you knew when you snapped that car!"

Well – what a thrill for Ian! The thieves were caught because of his picture, and in the newspapers the next

294

day was the photograph he had taken of the car and the men!

Ian was so proud that he couldn't stop talking about it.

"Fancy my little old camera taking a picture so valuable as that!" he kept saying. "What a fine picture I've got to put in my Car Book – the best and most exciting of the lot."

All the newspapers that printed Ian's car picture paid him a fee for it – and to his enormous surprise the boy soon had more money than he had ever had in his life!

"Almost one hundred pounds!" he said. "Well, I know what I'm going to do with it!"

I know too, don't you? He's going to buy a really magnificent camera now, for a Train Book. If ever you meet him, ask him to show you his Car Book – it's really very interesting indeed. *Especially* the last two pictures in the book – a big Italian car, shining in the sun – and a gleaming white car with a word showing clearly – POLICE.

A Spell
for a Lazy Boy

Tom was one of those boys who are always late for breakfast, late for school, last out at playtime, and behind in all their work. He was lazy and slow, and he just wouldn't be quick.

Now one day his father called to him and spoke kindly but sternly to him. "Listen, Tom. I am going to give you a reward if you try to alter yourself. You will be one of the useless people in the world when you grow up if you don't stir yourself up a bit, and really try not to be late or slow in everything. If for a whole week you are in time for everything, and even first at some things, and make a few runs in cricket, then I will give you a new bicycle."

"Oooh!" said Tom, his eyes opening

296

wide. All his friends had bicycles, but his father had never given him one because Tom never seemed to try hard at anything, and really didn't deserve one.

"Now, are you going to try hard?" said his father. Tom nodded, and his eyes shone. A new bicycle! One with a loud bell and a pump. Goodness, how fast he would go and what fun he would have with the other boys!

But although he had such a lovely reward offered to him, Tom didn't feel at all sure that he would be able to be first in anything, or even quick. He sat and thought about it.

"If I could get a spell to help me it would make things much easier," he

297

said to himself. "I'll go to the old woman who lives in the heart of the wood. People say that her grandmother was a witch, so maybe she knows a few spells."

Well, the old woman did. She gave Tom a little yellow pill in a box. "That's the finest spell I know for laziness," she said. "It gets into your arms and legs almost at once and makes them quick and strong and active. You'll be all right if you take that. But mind – if you get that bicycle because of my spell, I shall expect you to ride my errands on it twice a week!"

"Oh, I will, I will!" promised Tom, and ran off with the little yellow pill. He took it before he went to bed that night.

He fell asleep at once. The spell worked away inside him all the night. It got into his arms and legs, and into his fingers and toes. It awoke him in the morning.

Tom began to yawn and stretch himself as he always did. But his legs

gave him no time to do that – they leapt out of bed at once! Tom got a great surprise. But he soon had an even greater one. His arms began to work at top speed, and he found himself putting on pants and shirt and sweater and jeans faster than he had ever done before!

"Goodness!" said Tom, trying to stop his hands from putting on two shoes at once. But the spell was too strong – he couldn't stop himself at all. On went his shoes, and the laces were tied up in a twinkling.

Then his legs took charge of him again and raced him down the stairs at

299

top speed. He fell over the cat and bumped his head. He made such a noise that his father was cross.

"Tom! Is there any need to upset the whole household like this? What are you doing?"

Tom's legs had rushed him to the breakfast table, and now his hands were helping him to his breakfast, shaking cereal out of a packet, emptying milk and sugar on to his plate, and then making him eat so quickly that he almost choked.

Up and down to his mouth went the spoon, and poor Tom had no time to swallow one mouthful before the next was at his lips.

"Tom! Don't gobble like that!" said his mother. "Why are you in such a

300

hurry? Yesterday you were so lazy that you took hours over your meal, and today you gobble so fast that you choke. Behave yourself!"

It was the same with his boiled egg. His hand hacked off the top, and then the spoon dived in and out, and his other hand took bread and butter to his mouth at top speed, so that the egg and bread were finished in about half a minute.

"Tom!" said his father, laying down his paper. "Tom! If you think that this strange behaviour will make me give you a bicycle you are quite mistaken. You are being very silly. Sit back and be quiet whilst we finish our meal. I am ashamed of you."

But Tom could not sit back and be quiet whilst that spell was in him. His legs jumped up and ran him to his school satchel. His hands piled all his books in. They snatched his cap and jacket, and put them on. Then his legs rushed him to his father and mother to say goodbye, and then he tore out of the house and down the road. He felt rather sick. It wasn't at all good for him to gobble his breakfast like that.

"What's come over Tom?" said his mother in alarm. "You shouldn't have promised him a bicycle, Daddy, if it makes him behave like this!"

School was dreadful for poor Tom that morning. He was the first there, of course. The others didn't come for half an hour. But Tom's legs were not going to be lazy, and neither were his hands. They were soon hard at work, pulling up weeds in the school garden, piling them into a barrow, and running the barrow at top speed to the rubbish heap.

The headmaster was most amazed

302

when he arrived and saw what was happening. Could this be Lazy Tom? Could this be the slowest child in the school, weeding at top speed and wheeling the heavy barrow to the rubbish heap so quickly?

It was too good to be true.

Tom felt very tired when school began. He wasn't used to such hurrying and such hard work. He sank down into his seat thankfully. At any rate, he would get a rest now.

But, no, he didn't. His hands set to work at his sums and copied them down at such a speed that Tom could hardly see the figures. Then the spell began to work inside his head and his brain made him do the sums. He

couldn't think of anything else but sums. Usually he looked out of the window or round at the other children, lazing away his time. He couldn't do that this morning.

"You've done enough sums now, Tom," said the master in surprise. "You've done very well. I am pleased with you."

That made Tom glad, but he was feeling very alarmed now. This spell was much too powerful for him. He didn't like doing everything at such a pace. But it was just the same in the writing lessons.

The children were told to copy out a page in their history book in their best writing. At once Tom's fingers got to work and they wrote page after page. The master stared in astonishment. Tom usually wrote about half a page, but there he was turning over page after page, filling it with writing. Whatever could have happened?

When playtime came Tom's legs shot him off to the cloakroom to get his

lunch, and then shot him out to the playground, almost knocking over one or two children.

"What's the hurry now? What's the hurry?" they shouted, and gave him a push. "Stop rushing like this, Tom. It's not funny."

The children played games in the playground, and Tom ran about fast and dodged here and there, caught all the others easily, and knocked quite a lot over. The children didn't understand what was happening, and they were cross. Peter gave Tom a slap, and at once Tom's fists doubled themselves up and began to hit Peter.

305

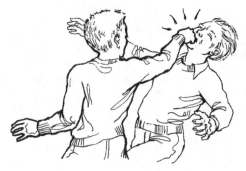

"A fight, a fight!" cried the boys, and came round. Tom didn't want to fight. He liked Peter. But his fists wouldn't stop lashing out at him. Then the master came up and spoke sternly and sent Tom indoors.

Tom sat down, breathless. He was tired and frightened. He wished he had never asked the old woman for a spell.

School went on for the rest of the morning, and in geography Tom drew six different maps, much to the astonishment of the teacher. He also learnt three pages of poetry, three times as much as any other pupil. He simply couldn't stop himself from working at top speed.

His legs raced him home for dinner, and his hands made him gobble again.

His mother was alarmed.

"Tom!" she said. "What has happened to you? Tell me, dear! It's almost as if you are under a spell!"

"Oh, Mother, I am!" said poor Tom. "I asked the old woman in the wood for a spell to make me quick instead of lazy and slow, and she gave me one, because I did so badly want to earn that bicycle. But the spell's too strong. Whatever am I to do?"

"I'll take you to the old woman at once," said his mother. "If she doesn't take away the spell you'll be tired out. Come along."

So they went to the wood. His mother had to run all the way, because Tom's legs didn't seem able to walk. The old woman laughed when she heard what the spell had been doing to him.

"I'm sorry," she said. "It only works like that on a really lazy boy, one who has never in his life tried to be quick or punctual or hard-working. I didn't think Tom was as bad as that."

307

"Please take the spell away," begged poor Tom. But the old woman couldn't.

"You'll have to put up with it for a day or two," she said, "but if after that you yourself try to be quick and early and work hard, the spell will gradually die away. But if you get lazy again I'm afraid it will come back, and you'll do everything at top speed, and annoy everyone, and get very tired."

So Tom put up with it for two days more, and then the spell seemed to die away. Tom tried hard to be early for everything, and to work hard after that, and he found it wasn't so difficult as it seemed. But, dear me, he had only to get lazy for a few minutes to start up that top-speed spell once more. You will be glad to know he got his bicycle!

Are you a lazy child? Tell your mother to let me know, and I'll see if I can get a top-speed spell for you and cure you, too!

When Mac was
a Shadow

Mac lived in a big town. It took a long time to get away from it and out into the country, so Mac used to go to the park to play.

"But you can't really play games like Red Indians in the park," he said to the others. "I mean – people wouldn't like us wriggling through the bushes, stalking one another. But it would be such fun to do things like that."

"Red Indians are babyish," said Tom, a big boy. "It's more fun to play at shadowing, or something like that."

"What's shadowing?" asked Mac. "It sounds good."

"Well – it's what the police do sometimes when they want to watch someone they suspect of something," said Tom. "They tell a man to follow the person around – act like a shadow – always there, but never noticed."

Mac thought about it. Shadowing could really be done anywhere. It might be fun. He asked Tom another question.

"Do you get into trouble if you shadow people for nothing – just for fun, I mean?"

"Not if you're a good shadower!" said Tom with a laugh. "They wouldn't even know you were there. Why – are you thinking of trying it?"

"I might," said Mac. "I shall think about it. It might make up for not playing Red Indians."

He did think about it, and he felt rather excited. Yes – it *would* be rather fun to pretend to be a policeman in plain clothes, and shadow someone – someone who wouldn't even guess that he, Mac, was behind him, watching where he went and what he did. He could pretend the man was an escaped prisoner or something.

So after tea the next evening Mac

310

slipped out by himself. He went into the town and looked round for someone to shadow. "I'll choose a nasty-looking fellow who *might* be somebody bad," he thought. "And I must be very, very careful that he doesn't spot me. If he does, he's won and I've lost. We'll both be playing a game together, but he won't know he is!"

He wandered along the street, keeping his eyes open for a shifty-looking fellow.

But everyone seemed to have a pleasant, kindly face. He stood outside a shop and watched.

Somebody came out of the shop and bumped into Mac. "Oh, sorry," he said. "I didn't see you there."

Mac rubbed his knee, where the man's heavy bag had knocked it. "It's all right," he said, and wondered if he should shadow this man. But he looked so jolly and friendly that Mac felt sure he wasn't anyone bad. So he let the man go and he was soon lost to sight.

Then someone else came by – and Mac decided at once that here was a

man to shadow. What a nasty-looking fellow! He looked dirty, his hat was pulled well over his face, a cigarette hung from the side of his mouth, and he slouched along with his hands in his pockets.

"Of course, he won't really be a bad lot at all," thought Mac, "but he looks one, so I'll shadow him."

The man slouched down the street. Mac slipped out of the doorway he stood in and walked after him. The man walked to the corner and turned it. Then he went into a doorway and stood looking at some books there. Mac

313

slipped into another doorway some way behind him and watched to see what the man would do next. Probably go into the shop and buy a book! But he didn't.

He set off again at a fair pace, and then, just as Mac came to the bookshop where the man had stood, the fellow stopped again and looked hard into another window. Mac slid into the doorway of the bookshop and looked at the shelf of books he had seen the man staring at.

He was very surprised when he saw them. They didn't seem at all the kind of books a man like that would study. They were a set of very expensive nature books.

"Oh, well – maybe he's interested in nature," thought Mac, and slipped out of the doorway as he saw the man walking on again.

It was a curious walk that the man took him – a walk that was interrupted by many starings into shop windows, and standing in doorways, looking out.

314

Mac began to feel puzzled. Surely the man didn't know he was following him?

And then, with quite a shock, Mac noticed what the man was doing. *He* was shadowing someone, too! He was following warily, slipping into doorways when the other man stopped to speak to someone, looking into windows if the other stopped to look at something, too. Mac strained his eyes in the half darkness to try and see what he was like.

"He's carrying a bag," he thought. "Why – it's the man who came out of that shop and bumped into me. His bag felt very heavy when it knocked my knee. Maybe there was money in it – people's wages or something!"

On went the man with the bag – on went the nasty fellow following him – and on went Mac, following too! But now it didn't seem a game any more.

What was the shadower going to do? Was he going to jump on the man with the bag when he came to a dark place, and knock him down, and steal his bag?

Mac felt quite sure something horrid was going to happen.

His heart began to beat fast. What could he do? He couldn't possibly stop the man – but neither could he warn the man with the bag! "I must do something, I really must," thought Mac desperately.

And then he saw Tom! He beckoned to him urgently.

Tom joined him in surprise. "I say, Tom," began Mac, in rather a breathless voice. "You'll have to help me. I came out to have a game of shadowing someone – like you told me, you know – and I chose that horrid-looking fellow,

some way in front there, to follow. Do you see him? Well – I've now discovered that *he's* shadowing someone, too – a man with a bag that I'm sure is full of money."

"Golly!" said Tom. "And he's going to knock him on the head when he comes to a dark spot!"

"Yes, I'm sure he is," said Mac. "So look here, Tom – you rush off now and find a policeman and tell him what is happening. It's no good telling the man with the bag, he might just laugh. The policeman will know what to do."

"Right," said Tom, and darted off up the street, passing the shadower and the man with the bag, too. He was soon out of sight, trying to find a policeman.

The man with the bag now walked steadily on. He met no one because he was now in a more deserted part of the town. He turned down a dark lane.

Immediately the shadower hurried a little and began to close in. Mac hurried, too, his heart thumping. The shadower was now almost up to the first man, and

Mac saw him raise his arm. Mac yelled loudly as the man with the bag dodged and fell to the ground. He hung on to his bag, though the shadower was tugging hard at it.

And then Tom appeared with a burly policeman! Oh, what a relief! Mac, Tom and the policeman surrounded the surprised thief. The man on the ground

got up and dusted himself down. He was feeling dazed – but he still had his bag of money firmly clutched in his hand.

Things happened quickly after that. The thief was arrested at once, and the policeman asked Tom, Mac and the man

with the bag to come along, too.

"Good boy, you," said the policeman to Tom. "Fetched me along just in the nick of time!"

"Oh, it was Mac here who sent me to find you," said Tom. "He was shadowing the shadower, and guessed what was going to happen."

Everyone was most astonished to hear this, especially the thief. "What? You were behind me all the time?" he growled. "What for?"

"Well – just for a game, actually," said Mac. "And then it suddenly changed from a game to the real thing."

"What a bit of luck for me!" said the man with the bag, who was now quite recovered. He patted Mac on the back. "Funny sort of thing to do, though – follow a man you don't know, just for a game. Are you going to be a policeman or a detective or something when you grow up?"

"Well – I might," said Mac, suddenly thinking that it might be a very good idea.

What a hero Mac was at school the next day! The boys crowded round to hear the story, and even the headmaster congratulated him on his adventure. And nicest of all was the reward that came to him from the man with the bag.

"One hundred pounds!" said Mac, hardly believing his eyes! "Well – no more shadowing for me – I'm going to buy a bike with this and ride out into the country each Saturday – and I'm going to play Red Indians there, and go stalking through the fields and hedges."

"Well, mind you don't stalk a bull, young Mac!" said Tom. "I shan't be there to fetch a policeman for you next time, you know!"

The Cat
With a Feathery Tail

There was once a cat who longed to catch the birds that flew about the garden. But the birds knew Tinker very well, and whenever he appeared, they always flew away.

It didn't matter where Tinker hid, the birds always found out. It was the blackbird who always seemed to see him hiding under the bushes.

"Beware, beware, beware!" the blackbird would cry in his loud voice. "Cat in the bushes! Cat in the bushes!"

Then all the birds would fly off at once, and Tinker would sit up and glare at the blackbird sitting at the top of the hazel tree.

Tinker's paws were velvety and soft. He made no noise when he ran. But

however softly he went, the birds always knew he was coming.

"Cat!" they cried to one another. "Chirrup, chirrup! Here's the cat!"

The other cats laughed at Tinker. "Birds are not so easy to catch as you think!" they said. "Leave them alone. They do you no harm. You have plenty of dinner to eat without worrying the birds."

But Tinker longed and longed to catch

324

the birds. He sat and thought for a long time how he might manage to get one.

Now the little boy he belonged to had a Red Indian hat. He sometimes wore it in the garden, and he looked very grand indeed when he did. It was made of green and yellow feathers, and was really magnificent.

Tinker saw this hat in the toy-cupboard one day when he was in the nursery, and an idea came into his clever mind.

"Suppose I get some of those feathers and tie them to my long tail," he thought. "Then I could lie down in the garden, curl my feathery tail over my body to hide me – and I would look like some kind of bird!"

The more he thought about this, the more he felt it was a splendid idea. So he bit out eight of the bright feathers and ran off with them to the garden shed. He got some of the string that the gardener kept there, and very cleverly managed to tie those feathers all along his tail. My, they did look funny, I can tell you!

325

Then out into the sunshine went Tinker, his long feathery tail dragging behind him. The cat went to the middle of the lawn and lay down. He curled his curious tail over his body, so that the feathers stood up and made him look like a peculiar kind of bird.

He kept quite still. Soon the blackbird saw him and cocked his head on one side as he balanced himself on the fence.

"Look at that, look at that!" called the blackbird. "What is it? A peacock? No! A kingfisher? No! Then what is it?"

The other birds flew down to look. They simply could not imagine what this curious bundle of feathers was. They felt sure it must be a new kind of bird.

326

They hopped a little closer. The sparrows put their brown heads on one side and watched carefully. The peculiar bird didn't move. It was very strange.

"Let's go right up to it and ask it what sort of bird it is," said the chaffinch. "I've never seen one quite like it before."

The cat was pleased. Aha, it would soon be able to jump up and catch five or six birds at once!

And then Fluffy, the next-door cat, jumped up on to the wall and caught sight of the peculiar bundle of feathers too. He was really astonished!

"Now what bird is that?" he thought. "I must go and see."

So he jumped down to the lawn and strolled over the grass. At once all the sparrows, the two chaffinches, the blackbird, and the thrush flew off in a fright.

"Beware, beware!" sang out the blackbird in his ringing voice. "Cat on the grass! Cat on the grass!"

Tinker peered through his feathers and saw Fluffy. What a nuisance! Fluffy had frightened away the birds. Perhaps if he lay quite still, Fluffy would go away, and then the birds would come back again.

So he lay as still as could be and only his feathery tail waved a little in the wind. Fluffy sat down to look at it.

He simply couldn't make out what kind of bird it was. He called to Paddy-Paws, the cat who lived in the house at the bottom of the garden.

"Paddy-Paws! Fetch Tibs and Tabby and come and look at this strange creature."

Paddy-Paws went off and fetched Tibs and Tabby. They were two grey tabbies. All four cats sat down and watched the bright feathery tail blowing in the wind. "Did you ever see a bird like this before?" said Fluffy.

"It doesn't seem to have a head," said Tibs.

"It seems to be mostly tail," said Tabby.

"It's not a bit afraid of us," said Paddy. "It doesn't fly away."

"I expect it would if we got a bit closer," said Fluffy. "Birds always do."

"Well, what about pouncing on it and catching it," whispered Tibs. "It doesn't seem to be moving. I think it is asleep. Let's try to catch it!"

"Right!" said Paddy. "Now – one – two – three – GO!"

All four cats leapt at the same time on to poor Tinker. He wasn't expecting that at all. He got a dreadful shock when he felt the four cats jump on to him. They dug their claws into him and Tibs bit him hard on the ear.

330

"Get away! You horrid things!" mewed Tinker, struggling hard and putting out all his twenty claws at once.

The cats were so excited that at first they didn't hear Tinker mewing. They scratched him hard. Feathers flew off his tail and danced about the lawn.

"Stop, stop!" cried Tinker, biting and scratching. "I'm a cat, not a bird! Leave me alone!"

The four cats leapt off Tinker in surprise. "Good gracious! It's Tinker!" said Fluffy.

"What have you dressed yourself up in feathers for?" said Tibs.

331

"Is this a new game or something?" said Tabby, disgusted. "What are you lying about the grass dressed up in yellow and green feathers for?"

"To catch the birds," said poor Tinker, licking his scratches. "You spoilt everything. I think you are silly, stupid, unkind things. You gave me a terrible shock when you jumped on me like that and dug your claws into me. Go away. I don't like you."

The four cats went away, laughing. The

blackbird sat on top of the fence and called to Tinker.

"Now you know what a bird feels like when a cat springs on it and digs her claws in! Serves you right, Tinker, serves you right!"

Tinker felt foolish. He washed himself and pretended to take no notice. But suddenly the little boy to whom Tinker belonged ran out into the garden. He had seen the torn feathers, and was very angry.

"You took them out of my Red Indian hat!" he cried. "You're a bad, bad cat! I shall smack you!"

And he did smack Tinker – slap, slap, slap! The surprised cat gave loud meows and ran away to hide. The blackbird sat on the top of the fence and called the news to all the other birds.

"The cat's getting smacked! Hurrah! The cat's getting smacked! Come and see-ee-ee! Come and see-ee-ee!"

And they all came to see-ee-ee. Poor Tinker! He never once tried to catch a bird after that!

Giggle and Hop
Get into Trouble

Dame Rap-Rap kept a school for pixies. It was a boarding-school, so they stayed there all the time, except when they went home for holidays. It was a very nice school and they all enjoyed it very much.

But there were two of the pixies who were real nuisances. If ever there was any trouble, Dame Rap-Rap was sure to find that it was because of Giggle and Hop. If the jam disappeared out of the cupboard, she would find that Giggle had been in the room two minutes before. If a window got broken, it would be because Hop had thrown his ball through it.

The worst of it was that it was very difficult to make sure that Giggle and

Hop were the two that caused all the trouble. They looked so good and sweet that Dame Rap-Rap could really hardly believe they could be so naughty.

Now one night Giggle and Hop woke up and looked out of the window. It was a moonlight night and Giggle thought it looked beautiful.

"Hop! Let's go and watch the frogs playing leapfrog tonight!" said Giggle. "They are having their races. I heard Jump say so today, when we passed the pond."

335

"But we aren't supposed to go out at night," said Hop, half afraid.

"What does that matter?" said Giggle, jumping out of bed. "Everyone is asleep. No one will know. Let's go!"

So they both crept out of the window, slid down the tree outside, and set off to the pond. The frogs were there on the bank, having their jumping match. It was great fun to watch!

"You ought not to be out of bed at this time of night," said a big frog suddenly. "I shall tell Dame Rap-Rap."

336

"Mean thing!" said Hop, and both the pixies ran off in a hurry. The frog kept his word and told Dame Rap-Rap, and she was very cross.

"Now, which of you was it who went to the frogs' jumping-match?" she asked the school next day. Naughty little Giggle and Hop didn't say a word. They just sat at their desks, looking sweet and good. Dame Rap-Rap looked at them and felt perfectly certain it couldn't be either Giggle or Hop. So she didn't find out who it was at all.

Giggle and Hop thought it would be fine fun to slip out again one night. So when they heard the moths were holding a honey-supper in the wood,

337

they slipped out of bed, down the tree
outside the window, and went to join the
moths.

They were all sipping honey and
telling each other the news. They flew
softly here and there and their big
plumy feelers waved to and fro as they
chattered. Giggle and Hop tried to join
in, and they each took a big pot of honey

338

for themselves.

But the moths were angry.

"You haven't been invited!" they said. "Go home! You belong to Dame Rap-Rap's school, we know! We shall tell her tomorrow how you came here and took our honey. What are your names?"

But the pixies wouldn't tell the moths. They fled back to the school and went to bed. And in the morning Dame Rap-Rap had a letter saying that two of her pupils had slipped out the night before. She was very cross.

She simply *couldn't* find out who the naughty pixies were. Giggle and Hop just sat and looked as sweet as possible, and seemed quite shocked when Dame Rap-Rap said that SOMEONE had been out in the woods the night before.

Well, when they heard that the field mice were having a dance at the edge of the cornfield, they winked at one another and made up their minds to go there too, that very night.

So off they went, and weren't they pleased to see a fine spread of cheesecake, bacon rind sandwiches, and wobbly jellies set out for the fieldmice to eat. Giggle and Hop danced a dance together and then began to eat the cakes. They were really delicious.

They were just finishing a jelly when Pitter, the head fieldmouse, came scampering up. "What are you doing?" he cried. "You don't belong to our party! Go home! How dare you take our food!"

"We thought you would be proud if we came to the party," said Giggle. "It isn't often that pixies come to dance with the fieldmice!"

"You go home at once!" cried the fieldmouse angrily. "You go to Dame Rap-Rap's school, we know. Well, we'll tell her about you! You'll be punished!"

"Oh no, we shan't!" cried Hop, and he snatched another cake. The fieldmouse was so angry that he rushed at the pixie and knocked him right over. Then up came all the other fieldmice, and the pixies saw that they must run away.

They ran – but the mice ran after them! "Quick!" cried Giggle. "Hide!"

340

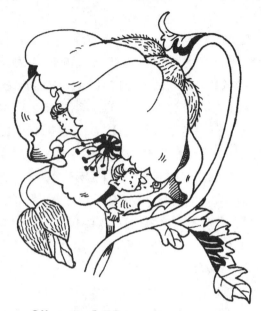

"Where?" cried Hop.

"In a poppy!" cried Giggle. The red poppies were standing here and there at the edge of the field. In a second the two pixies each climbed a green stalk, parted the red silky petals and hid themselves inside a poppy. The fieldmice raced along below and passed them, for they had not seen what the pixies were doing.

"Good!" cried Hop, when he saw that they were safe. "Come along! We'd better get back to school."

341

Off they ran, and were soon in bed. They didn't know that they were quite black with pollen off the poppies. You know what a black middle the poppies have, don't you? Well, all the black had come off on to the pixies!

They hadn't been in bed long when a fieldmouse came knocking at the school door. In great alarm Mrs Rap-Rap put on her dressing gown, and went down to open the door.

How angry she was when the fieldmouse told her that two of her pixies had been to the dance by the cornfield!

"Oh, really!" she said. "Well, I'll just find out this time who it is. I'll wake the whole school up and find out if everyone is here. Thank you, Fieldmouse!"

Dame Rap-Rap rang the school bell. All the pixies woke up in alarm. Dame Rap-Rap went in and out of the bedrooms calling, "Put on your dressing-gowns and go into the hall! Put on your dressing-gowns and go into the hall!"

342

In five minutes every pixie was there. Dame Rap-Rap counted them. Dear, dear! no one was missing after all. But then she looked very carefully at Giggle and Hop. They were *black!*

"Why are you so dirty?" she asked sternly. "Your faces are black, your hands are black – and dear me, your nightsuits, under your dressing-gowns, are black too! Have you been in the coal cellar?"

"No, Dame Rap-Rap," said the pixies at once.

"I know what the black is," cried little

Twinkle. "It's the black from the middle of poppies! I got some on my nose yesterday!"

"Oh!" said Dame Rap-Rap, and she stared sternly at the two trembling pixies. "And poppies grow by the cornfield – and the dance is held there tonight – and two pixies went – and were chased away and hid – and I guess they hid in the poppies and got black!

And I guess, too, that those pixies were *you,* Giggle and Hop! Come with me at once!"

They had to go with Dame Rap-Rap – and dear me, she hadn't got her name for nothing. All the other pixies stood and listened. "Rap-rap-rap!" they heard. "Rap-rap-rap!"

And if you'd like to get yourselves as black as Giggle and Hop, just go and put your nose inside a poppy. You'll soon see how it was that the pixies got so dirty!

Michael's
New Belt

Michael was very proud of his new leather belt. It had little brass studs on it half-way round and a rather grand buckle.

"See my belt?" he said to the other boys. "My uncle gave me that. He brought it back from Canada with him. I guess this is the kind of belt that cowboys wear on a ranch over there."

The other boys thought it was fine. They fingered it and patted the brass studs. "Wish I had one like that," said William, the head of the class. Michael was very proud to hear him say that.

Michael was very careful of his new belt. He didn't wear it every day. He kept it for Sundays, or for the days he went to see his granny or his aunts. Then he would buckle the new belt

round his jeans, with the brass studs and buckle shining brightly, and set off proudly.

One day he went to see his granny. He stayed to dinner with her and then set off to walk home. He had on his new belt, of course, and Granny had admired it for the twentieth time.

"I suppose you wouldn't lend it to me to wear when I go to London next week," she said solemnly.

Michael laughed. "Oh, Granny – you

346

wouldn't want to wear a belt like mine, you know you wouldn't – but I would lend it to you if you really wanted it. I wouldn't lend it to any boy or girl though! It's much too precious!"

He went off home with two little ginger cakes Granny had baked for his tea. And on the way home he heard someone shouting so loudly that he stopped in surprise. Who was shouting? Michael was in the fields and he couldn't see anyone about at all. The shouting went on and on. "Help! Help, me! Can't you see me? I'm up here. *Up here!* Up the tree!"

Then Michael looked up, and there, a good way up a tall tree on the other side of the hedge, he saw a boy. The tree was bare, and Michael could see him easily. He stared in surprise.

"I say! Help me, won't you?" yelled the boy.

"Why? What's the matter? Can't you climb down?" yelled back Michael, going nearer the tree.

"No. I've got stuck somehow. And

347

now I'm frightened," said the boy, sounding almost as if he were going to cry.

"Why did you climb so high?" called Michael.

"There's a bull in this field and he ran at me," shouted back the boy. "I just had time to shin up this tree, and I can tell you I climbed faster than I've ever climbed in my life! Now I'm stuck – and I'm awfully afraid of falling. I feel giddy."

"I'll come up and help you down," said Michael. He kept a look-out for the bull, which didn't seem to be anywhere around, and then began to climb up the tree. He soon reached the boy.

"Look – can't you put your foot down to this branch?" he said to the boy. "What's your name? I don't seem to have seen you before."

"I'm Robert Trent," said the boy. "No – I can't put my foot down to the branch. I tell you, I'm scared. I think I'm going to be sick."

Michael looked at him. He did look rather green.

"You're not *really* afraid of falling, are you?" he said anxiously. "Here – hold on to me until you feel a bit better." The boy wouldn't even hold on to Michael. He wouldn't let go his hold of the branch he was on.

"Isn't there a ladder I can get down by?" he said desperately. "Surely there's one at the farm. I know I shall fall soon."

"I'll go and run to the farm for help,"

said Michael, beginning to climb down again. But the boy cried out at once: "No! Don't leave me! I shall fall down the tree if you do, I know I shall. Stay with me."

"But that's silly," said Michael, sensibly. "How can I possibly go and get help if you won't let me leave you?"

"I don't know," said the boy, looking greener than ever. "I do feel awful. I daren't even open my eyes now, because I know I shall feel giddy if I do."

Michael looked down the tree. It was a long, long way to fall. He began to feel frightened for the boy. Suppose he did fall? He might be killed – or at least break a leg or an arm.

The boy spoke again, his eyes still shut. "Have you got a rope, by any chance? So that you could tie me to this branch? If you could do that I'd feel safer and I'd let you go and fetch help."

"No, I haven't got a rope," said Michael. And then a thought struck him. He hadn't a rope – but he had got a fine, strong leather belt!

He looked down at his belt. He didn't want to lend it to anyone, not even to Robert. It would probably be rubbed against the tree – some of the brass studs might come out. No, he couldn't think of lending it to this foolish boy.

But Michael was a kindly boy, and he didn't go on thinking like this for long. He suddenly unbuckled his belt and slipped it off his jeans.

"I'll buckle you to the branch with

351

my belt," he said. "That will keep you safe. It's very good, strong leather."

But the belt wasn't long enough to buckle the boy to a branch. So Michael did the next best thing – he buckled the belt loosely to a near-by bough, and told Robert to slip his arm through it. Then he tightened the belt over the boy's arm. "There!" he said.

352

"Now even if you do feel yourself falling my belt will hold you up. You needn't be afraid any more."

"Oh, that's a wonderful idea," said the boy, gratefully. "I feel better already. Thanks very much."

"I'll go down now and get a ladder or something," said Michael, and he shinned quickly down the tree, glad that he had a better head than Robert for climbing! He ran off towards the farm.

It was a long time before he could find anyone to help him. The farmer and his wife were at market. The men were at work in different places. At last Michael found one who listened to his tale.

"What – a boy up a tree and can't get down!" said the man. "What sort of a boy is that? He's not worth bothering with!"

"But I know he'll fall if I don't get help," said Michael. "Where's a ladder? Can I borrow one?"

"No! A youngster like you can't

carry a great heavy ladder to put half-way up a tree," said the man. "Wait until I've finished this job and I'll come myself."

So Michael had to wait impatiently until the man finished his work. Then, not hurrying himself at all, he went with Michael to the tree in the field where the bull was. But Robert wasn't there! He had gone!

"This is the tree," said Michael. "But the boy's gone! How odd!"

"Look here," said the man, "did you make this all up, just to play a trick? Because if you did, I'll..."

"No – I really didn't," said Michael

354

hurriedly. "Please believe me, I even lent the boy my best leather belt to hang on to, and tied up my jeans with a bit of string – look."

"Well – you won't see your leather belt any more, that's certain," said the man, and went off. Michael stood there alone feeling very upset. Was the man right? Had he really lost his belt for good?

He saw a man in the field, leading the bull with a stick which he had fastened to a ring at the end of the bull's nose. He called to him.

"I say! Did you see a boy up a tree here frightened of falling?"

"Yes. I saw him when I came to get the bull," shouted back the man. "Silly youngster, climbing so high he's scared of falling. I got him down all right."

"Where did he go?" asked Michael. "Did he say anything about a leather belt I lent him?"

"No, he didn't," said the man. "He fastened one round his waist – a beauty it was – and off he went."

"Oh," said Michael. He was upset and disappointed. He had helped the boy – and all the return he got was to lose his belt, and not have a single word of thanks!

He went home and told his mother all about it. "If I meet that boy again I'll fight him!" he said. "He might at least have waited under the tree until I came back, and given me my belt. My beautiful belt! Mother, I'll never lend anyone my belt again – I won't lend anyone *any*thing again. I won't even help people in trouble."

"Now, that's not like you, Michael," said his mother. "You mustn't think

bad of people until you are certain they have done something wrong or unkind. And how foolish to change yourself from a kind, generous boy into an unkind, selfish one just because somebody has behaved badly to you!"

"Oh, well – I expect you're right as usual, Mother," said Michael. "I'll be sensible. But you don't know how upset I am about my belt."

Now, a week after that, Michael went shopping in the next town with his mother. As he was walking down the road, a car suddenly stopped just by

357

him and a head popped out. A voice called excitedly:

"I say, I say! Aren't you the boy who lent me your lovely belt up that tree?" And there was Robert looking out of the car window! Michael nodded, looking rather surly. The boy got out of the car and ran to him.

"A man got me down from the tree after you'd gone. I put on your belt to keep it safe, and then I went off to look for you – but I lost my way and never found you. And ever since I've worried and worried as I was afraid you'd think I'd gone off with it and never meant to give it back!"

Michael didn't know *what* to say!

358

His mother came to the rescue. "Michael is always lending things to others, and he always gets them back."

A man looked out of the car. "Is this the boy who helped Robert?" he said. "We've been making enquiries about him all over the place. Thank you, sonny, for doing your best for him. He's an idiot to climb trees – he always feels giddy."

"Here's your belt," said Robert, taking a parcel out of the car. "I've carried it about with me ever since last week, hoping I'd see you somewhere. Dad, can we take him to the circus with us? Can he come now?"

"Well – we must ask his mother," said Robert's father. You can guess what Michael's mother said.

"Of course he can come," she said. "Do you mean now, this very minute? Oh, what a surprise for you, Michael!"

It certainly was. In a flash he was in the car, sitting beside Robert, speeding off to the circus. What a wonderful time he had!

And now, of course, Robert and Michael are quite inseparable – in fact, Michael's mother says she never sees one without the other! And will you believe it, Michael lends his belt to Robert whenever he asks him to!

Sailor Jim's Telescope

Sailor Jim had a telescope. He put it on a stand down by the sea-wall, and anyone could have a look through it for ten pence.

"We can see the lighthouse as if it was as near as the sea-wall!" said Peter.

"And you can see that bird far out to sea just as if it was flying by your nose!" said Lucy.

"And if I look at that far-off boat I can even see who's in it!" said James. "It's my cousin Harry and his friend Don!"

Sailor Jim liked the children. He gave them a free peep through his telescope every Saturday morning if they could come and tell him that they had had good marks at school.

And one day George came to tell him a very good piece of news indeed. "Sailor Jim – what do you think!" he said. "I've won a scholarship!"

"You don't mean it!" said Sailor Jim. "Well, well, what brains you must have! Now you tell me what you'd like from me for a reward, and you can have it! A sail in my boat? A fishing-trip with me? What would you like to have?"

"Sailor Jim, I suppose you wouldn't lend me your telescope for just one day, would you?" asked George. "My little sister's ill in bed, and she would so love to have your telescope to look through for a little while. She isn't allowed to read. She could look at the birds in the trees, and the sheep far away on the hill – she'd love that!"

"But I wanted to give *you* a reward, not your sister," said Sailor Jim. "Surely you would like to go on a fishing-trip with me, George?"

"Oh, *yes* – better than anything," said George. "But I know how Pat would like your telescope for just one day.

She's often said so."

Sailor Jim didn't know what to say. He really didn't want to part with his telescope for a whole day, especially as there were many people visiting his town now – he would lose a lot of money. But still, he had said that George could ask for what he wanted.

"Right," he said at last. "You can take it tomorrow. But be careful of it, won't you?"

George was delighted. How pleased Pat would be! She would feel better at once.

He called for it the next morning and proudly took it off to his sister. She squealed with delight when she saw it

and held out her hands. Soon it was propped up on her bed, and she was looking through it.

"The sheep look so big!" she said. "And now I can see the two little foals properly in the next field. And I can see the rooks pecking up grubs and the shepherd's dog scratching himself. It's like magic! Everything is so near!"

After tea her mother left her by herself with the telescope. George was out in the garden reading. Pat settled down to look through the telescope. She turned it on Mr Land's farm and watched the hens and the ducks there. She turned it on the big field and saw the cows walking through the gate to be milked.

364

"And now I'll look at that dear little thatched cottage," she said to herself. The cottage was near a privately owned railway line, and steam trains often went by. Pat could watch the trains with the telescope as well as have a look at the cottage, with its thatched roof and tall hollyhocks.

"It's rather like a fairy-tale cottage," she thought. "I wonder where the old lady is who lives there? Perhaps she is still having her tea indoors. Oh – here comes a train!"

She heard the rumble and then saw the smoke from the steam engine. The

365

train chugged by the cottage, spitting out smoke and a trail of sparks from its funnel.

It soon disappeared. Pat looked at the cottage through the telescope again. She saw something on the thatched roof. What could it be?

It moved about. Was it a white bird? No – it couldn't be. It grew bigger. It was – yes, it must be – smoke!

"*Smoke!*" said Pat in alarm. "Smoke on the old cottage's thatched roof! A spark from the engine must have blown there – and it's set light to the dry thatch – the straw has caught alight. Oh dear – the cottage will be burnt down!" The little girl raised her voice and shouted: "Mummy! MUMMY! Quick, come here!"

Her mother and George came running up at once. "Look," cried Pat, pointing out of the window. "A spark has set the roof of that cottage on fire. It's burning. Call the fire engine, quick! I saw it through the telescope George brought me."

Mummy flew downstairs to the telephone. She got on to the fire station at once and told them the news.

"Thanks, madam. The old thatched cottage near the railway, you say? We'll be there in three minutes!"

And so they were! Pat watched the whole thing through the telescope in the greatest excitement. The fire engine raced up. The firemen leapt down. A hose was unrolled, and water began to play on the burning thatch. And in the middle of it all an old lady came angrily out of her cottage.

367

"What are you doing? What is the meaning of this?" she cried. The firemen pointed to the smoking roof where the flames were now almost out.

"Your roof was on fire, missus," said one. "Just got the warning in time."

"Who gave the warning?" said the old lady, astonished.

"A little girl called Pat, who lives up in that house over there," said the fireman, pointing. "She told her mother and her mother telephoned through to us – and here we are!"

"Thank you, thank you," said the old

lady. "I must tell my son, and he will go and thank the little girl."

Who do you suppose her son was? *Sailor Jim.* Wasn't that strange? He was so glad to know that his mother's cottage had been saved that he walked up to George's house that evening and asked to see Pat.

"I'd like to see the little girl who noticed that my mother's roof was on fire," he said to Pat's mother. "I want to thank her."

So up he went into Pat's bedroom – and the very first thing he saw there was his own telescope! He stared at it in astonishment.

"How did you get this?" he asked, picking it up.

"George brought it home for just one day for me to look through – my brother George," said Pat. "And it was when I

369

was looking through it after tea that I saw the roof of that cottage smoking. Wasn't it a good thing I had the telescope?"

"It was," said Sailor Jim. "A very good thing indeed. And what a very, *very* good thing I lent it to George because he won a scholarship!"

"Oh! Are you Sailor Jim?" cried Pat. "George, George, come quickly, here's Sailor Jim!"

George came in and looked astonished to see Sailor Jim. "Have you come for the telescope?" he asked.

"George, it was Sailor Jim's mother's cottage I saw burning through *his* telescope!" cried Pat. "Isn't it strange – just like a house-that-Jack-built story!"

Sailor Jim laughed. "This is the boy who won a scholarship. This is the man who wanted to give him a reward. This is the telescope he lent him. This is the little girl who used it. That's the cottage she saw burning – and here's the man who came to say thank you for saving his mother's home."

370

"Oh, Sailor Jim – I'm glad your telescope saved your mother," said George. "What a good thing I asked for it!"

"Yes – and I'm giving you something else now," said Sailor Jim. "Another reward! Will you both come out fishing with me as soon as this little lady is better?"

"I'll be better tomorrow. I will! I will!" cried Pat.

"You get better by next Saturday and we'll go," said Sailor Jim. So Pat is going to get well by then, and off they will all go together to catch plenty of fish for Saturday's supper.

It's strange how things happen, isn't it? You simply never know!

"I Dare
You To!"

"I dare you to!" said Geoffrey to Bill.

The two boys were standing outside old Mr White's cottage. It had a funny old-fashioned bell-pull, and when you pulled the handle you could hear a bell jangling somewhere in the little house.

"Go on – pull it! I dare you to!" said Geoffrey. He was always daring somebody to do something silly – and nearly all the boys were silly enough to take his dares.

"Pooh – I would dare a lot more than just pulling a bell!" said Bill, scornfully. He ran up to the front door and gave the bell-rope a terrific pull. To his horror it came away in his hand, and at the same time there was a loud jangling noise inside the house.

372

"Run!" shouted Geoffrey. "You've broken the rope, you idiot! Run!"

Bill ran for all he was worth. Old Mr White was a hot-tempered fellow, and he was getting very tired of mischievous children who tugged at his bell-pull. Whatever would he say to somebody who broke it?

Bill fled down the street, feeling ashamed of himself for running away. But that afternoon, when Geoffrey told the other boys how Bill had taken his dare, and not only pulled at old Mr White's bell but had actually tugged the rope in two, Bill found himself quite a hero! He forgot that he had been ashamed of running away, and he began to boast.

"That was nothing! I'd take a bigger dare than that!"

"I dare you to ride down Langham Hill without your bike brakes on!" said Geoffrey at once.

"Right!" said Bill.

"Don't be such as ass," said Derek, the head-boy of the class. "You'll have an accident. That hill is too steep to ride down without brakes on."

"There's hardly any traffic down that hill," said Bill. "I shan't have an accident, don't worry. I've got all my wits about me. It'll be great sailing down there at top speed."

The boys all went to see him take the dare and ride down Langham Hill. It really was a very steep hill indeed, but perfectly straight, and had a good level of stretch at the end. Very little traffic used it, because it was too steep.

374

It certainly looked quite safe.

"Here goes!" said Bill, and got on his bike.

Whoooooooosh! Down he went, twenty miles an hour, thirty, forty ...!

"As fast as a motor-bike!" said the boys, admiringly. "Look at him!"

Bill sped down the hill, enjoying the wind in his hair and the swiftness of his bicycle. What a ride! He came up on the level stretch and the bicycle sped along there too, and then gradually slowed down.

Bill leapt off and waved to the boys who were now running down the hill towards him. Then he rode to meet them, pedalling leisurely along.

"Jolly good!" said Geoffrey. "What did it feel like?"

"Grand," said Bill. "I'd do it again any time. Anyone want to dare me again?"

"We'll think of another dare for you, not the same one," said Geoffrey. "There's nobody as brave as you, Bill."

"And nobody as silly!" thought Derek, the head-boy, but he didn't say it out loud. Bill was so pleased with all the back-thumpings and praise he was getting that he certainly wouldn't like being called silly.

Well, that was the beginning of many other dares. Bill was dared to ride home one night without lights, and he did, though he met the policeman and was rather scared when he was shouted at.

He rode all the way home from school holding on to the tail of a van because Geoffrey dared him to. The van-man saw him and yelled at him, but Bill wasn't going to spoil his dare, and he didn't lose hold of the van till

he came to the road where he lived. Ha
– he'd show the boys how brave he
was. He was Dare-devil Bill, afraid of
nothing.

Certainly Bill was a very clever
cyclist. He was always in perfect
control of his bicycle, which was a real
beauty. It had cost nearly one hundred
pounds, and had been a very special
birthday present from his mother and
father and grandmother. Its brakes
were perfect, its lamp was beautiful,
and its red rear-light always shone out
splendidly.

Bill could ride so slowly on it that it

377

almost looked as if he were going to fall off, but he never did. He could ride sitting on the saddle, with his feet up on the handlebars to steer instead of his hands. There was no end to the tricks he could do.

"There aren't many dares left for Dare-devil Bill," said the boys at last. "He's done everything."

"I bet he wouldn't dare to ride across the traffic lights when they showed red," said Harry. "Nobody would dare to do that."

"Nobody would be idiot enough," said Derek.

"Hi, Bill!" shouted Geoffrey. "I've got another dare for you. Would you dare to ride against the traffic-lights – go across when they show red instead of green?"

"You bet!" said Bill at once. "That's easy. Which traffic lights? Choose difficult ones, or it will be no fun."

"All right. Ride over the crossing at the end of the High Street," said Geoffrey. "On the way home from

378

morning school. We'll watch! I bet you'll be nippy enough to get over before anyone knows what you're doing."

Bill was there at the High Street crossing, after morning school, standing with his bike, waiting for the lights to turn red. The boys stood a little way off, watching. Many people were walking up and down the pavement – women shoppers, hurrying men, and small children on their way home to dinner. None of them guessed what Bill was going to do.

The lights turned red against him. Bill leapt on his bike. He rode straight across the road against the lights, with cars hooting at him and drivers

shouting. He was nippy. He kept his wits about him as usual. He was soon at the other side, perfectly safe, and he sailed off into a side-street, in case by any chance a policeman had seen him riding against the lights.

He didn't hear a crash behind him. He didn't hear screams. He didn't see the crowd that gathered round a little girl on the ground. He rode home whistling cheerfully, thinking what a clever, courageous fellow he was.

He went to school that afternoon as usual, expecting to be praised for his daring and patted on the back. He

380

looked for Geoffrey – but Geoffrey wasn't there. He looked at the other boys and grinned cheerfully. But nobody grinned back. They boys looked away from him. Nobody spoke to him.

"What's up?" said Bill, puzzled.

"Haven't you heard what's happened?" said Derek. "When you rode across the road, against the lights, a car jammed on its brakes so as to avoid you – and it swung across the pavement and knocked down a little girl. She was taken to hospital."

Bill went white. "Who was it?" he said, almost in a whisper. "Anyone I know?"

"Yes. It was Geoffrey's little sister, Bets," said Derek. Then he burst out angrily at Bill.

"You and your idiotic dares! You

381

think you're so clever, don't you, showing off all the stupid things you can do, breaking all the rules of the road, and getting off scot-free yourself! Look at you – thinking you're so wonderful – and that poor little Bets dying in hospital! You're a worm – no, you're even worse than a worm."

Bill sat down suddenly. He felt ill. Bets – little Bets dying in hospital – why, she had only come to tea the day before yesterday, and he had shown her how to do a jigsaw puzzle. He was fond of Bets, with her round red face and golden curls.

"It isn't true," said Bill with a groan. "Say it isn't true."

"It *is* true," said Derek. "That's why

382

Geoffrey isn't here this afternoon. He's at the hospital with his mother and father. Imagine what he feels like! It's all because he dared you to do that silly trick that this awful thing has happened to his sister. But you're all right – nothing's happened to *you*! You can still go on taking silly dares, and doing idiotic things, and bringing trouble to other people."

"Don't," said Bill, feeling sick.

"We're all to blame," said Harry. "We all enjoyed seeing him take the dares – and we patted him on the back like anything. We should have smacked his head instead. Poor little Bets! I keep thinking of her. She – she was right under the car, and she screamed."

Bill got up, looking as white as a sheet. He went straight to the headmaster's study and walked in without knocking. The headmaster looked up.

"Sir," said Bill, "I'm in great trouble. It's about Geoffrey's little sister, Bets. Please, sir she's not dying, is she?"

"I don't know," said the Head. "She's badly hurt. I can only hope it wasn't one of the boys of this school who rode against the lights and caused the accident."

"I was the boy," said Bill clutching at the desk. "What shall I do sir? Tell me what to do. Tell me *some*thing!" The headmaster looked at Bill in horror. He got up and spoke sternly.

"The first thing to do is to report to the police. Come with me?"

That was a terrible afternoon. In a dream, Bill went to the police-station and gave all the details of the stupid dare to a stern policeman. He went home, and his mother listened in terror and distress to the tale. His father was telephoned for and came home too.

"Mother, what about Bets? Will she die?" said Bill desperately.

His father telephoned the hospital. "Bets is out of danger," he said thankfully. "She'll recover – but she has a broken arm and leg besides cuts

384

and bruises. Oh, Bill – how could you do this? What unhappiness you've brought on yourself and us, and little Bets and her family!"

"I can never, never make up to Bets for this," thought Bill. "I must go and see her every day at the hospital. I must take her flowers and toys and dolls, and everything I possibly can. But where can I get the money? I've only about twenty pence."

He got the money. He got a great deal of money.

Because, you see, he sold his magnificent bicycle and spent every penny on Bets. She's better now,

385

though she still limps a little. She loves Bill for being so kind.

Bill can't understand why Bets is fond of him. He thinks she should hate him – and Geoffrey too.

"After all, we nearly killed you between us," he tells Bets. "That was the most terrible afternoon of my life, I can tell you; it's changed me into a different person altogether!"

And a very good thing too! What do *you* think?

Adventure
for Two

"Coming with me in the car?" called
Daddy to Philip and Mary. "I'm just
going down to see old Mrs Blakey."

"Oh, is she ill?" said Mary. Her daddy
was a doctor and went to see ill people
every day.

"No, not ill. She's sprained her ankle,
that's all," said Daddy. "I'm just going
to have a look at it – and then I rather
thought I'd go to the bakery and have
one of those chocolate ice-creams of
theirs. But you know how I hate eating
ice-creams alone."

"Oooh, Daddy! Of course we'll come!"
said Philip. He came running out of the
playroom with Mary. "You're a great
Daddy! You always tell us when you're
going ice-creaming!"

They went to get their coats. Their father went out to get his car. He brought it into the front drive.

Philip and Mary came running out. "I'll go in the front now, and you can be there coming back," said Mary to Philip. In they got, and off went the car. Down the drive, out into the road, and up the hill. Down the hill and round the corner – and there was old Mrs Blakey's house, with its thick yew hedge all round the front garden.

"Now you just look after my car for me whilst I'm in the house," said Daddy, "then I shan't need to lock it up. I always have to if there's nobody in it, because my precious case of medicines might be stolen."

"Oh, yes," said Philip. "And some of them are very poisonous, aren't they?"

Daddy went up the path to the house. The children sat in the car, looking at the thick yew hedge. Mary got out.

"I just want to look at the hedge," she said to Philip. "It's so very, very thick. Why, it's thick enough to get

388

right into the middle of it!"

Philip got out, too. They had always liked old Mrs Blakey's thick yew hedge. Mary parted the green boughs and looked into the depths of the dark hedge.

"Philip!" she said. "Look! There's a kind of passage going right along the middle of the hedge!"

Philip looked. It did really seem like a passage! The leaves there had dried and fallen off, and the middle of the hedge was empty and bare.

"We could almost go along it," said Philip. "Mary – shall we just get into it for a minute? I believe if we were in the very middle nobody could possibly see us! What a wonderful hiding-place it would make!"

"Let's hide from Daddy!" said Mary at once. "That *would* be fun! He'd come out and look for us – and we wouldn't be there!"

"And we could say something in a very deep, hollow kind of voice," said Philip. "It would make him jump! Come on, Mary, before he comes out."

It was easy to squeeze into the thick yew hedge. Once in the centre the branches closed firmly round them, and nobody could see them.

"But I've got a fine peep-hole, Mary – have you?" asked Philip. "I can see Daddy's car through it."

"Yes. I've got a peep-hole, too – between some leaves," said Mary. "Philip – supposing somebody comes by – had we better keep still and quiet?"

"Yes," said Philip. "We can't give our hiding-place away!"

"I can hear someone coming now," said Mary, and she looked through her peep-hole. "It's Jimmy White!"

Jimmy passed by, whistling cheerfully. Philip and Mary giggled. They longed to say "Beware, Jimmy!" in a deep, peculiar voice, but they knew Jimmy

391

well enough to know that he would at once go to look in the hedge for the voice!

"Now there's a woman coming," whispered Philip. "I don't know her."

The woman passed, walking quickly. The children sat quite still in their hiding-place. The passer-by didn't know anyone was so near her!

Nobody came for a little while. Then Philip heard soft footsteps. He peeped out.

"Two men, Mary," he whispered. "Aren't they walking quietly!"

The men came up to the car – but they didn't walk past. They stopped just by it. The children held their breath in case their hiding-place should be discovered.

"No one about," said one man in a very low voice. "Whose car's this? It's got a case inside."

"It's Dr Fenton's car," said the other man in such a low voice that the children could hardly hear him. "That will be his case. There will be valuable

drugs in there. Any chance of getting them?"

"Better try now, whilst there's no one to see," said the first man. He wrenched the front door of the car open and put his hand in quickly. In a second he had taken the case and had shut the door quietly.

Then the two men moved off quickly, walking very softly.

The children had seen all this, and were absolutely thunderstruck. Two robbers! Thieves who had dared to open their father's car and take his case – in full daylight, too! Well, you read of such things in the newspapers – but they never, never happened under your nose like this!

"Mary!" said Philip, finding his tongue at last. "We didn't do a thing. We never even shouted."

"I couldn't," said Mary. "It all happened so quickly. What are we going to do? Daddy's case is gone."

"And we were supposed to be in charge of it," said Philip, horrified at the thought. "Goodness – we were pretty feeble, Mary. If only we'd just given one shout those men would have shot off at once, without even opening the car."

"Yes, but it all happened so *quickly*," said Mary, almost in tears. "I couldn't say a word. I did try, but I couldn't. Let's get out of this hedge and tell Daddy."

At that very moment they heard the front door slam, and their father came briskly down the path.

"Now what about our ice-creams?" he called, as he got to the gate.

Philip and Mary were just climbing out of the hedge. They looked untidy and were covered with little bits and pieces. They looked so very solemn that their father was surprised.

"I say – did you *have* to climb into that dirty old hedge?" he said, opening his car. Then he stopped and stared.

"Good gracious – where's my case gone?"

"Daddy, it's been stolen," said Philip. "Oh, Daddy, it was our fault. We were in the hedge when the men came by and we ..."

"Now begin at the beginning and tell me everything," said Daddy, seeing at once that something serious had happened. So the two children told him everything: how they had got into the hedge, how people had come by, and the two men had come and talked, and then had stolen the case.

"Did they see you?" asked Daddy. "Did they know you were there?"

"Oh no," said Philip. "But we saw *them* all right. We know exactly what they are like and how they are dressed. If we saw them again we'd know them."

"Very well, then – hop quickly into the car," said Daddy. "I'll go to the police-station and collect a policeman in plain clothes, and we'll drive slowly round and about the streets. Maybe we'll see those men again!"

This was all very exciting indeed. The children got into the car, and Daddy drove off. He went first to the police-station, then quickly told what had happened, and was given an extra passenger – a policeman dressed in ordinary clothes.

"They'll have wrapped up that case of yours in brown paper by now, sir," said the policeman. "No good looking for the case – have to look for a large brown-paper parcel, or a suitcase big enough to have put your case in. They

397

wouldn't be foolish enough to carry your bag openly for long. Good thing these youngsters of yours noticed what the men were like!"

The car drove slowly down one street and up another. "There are two men," said the policeman suddenly. "Sitting on that seat, sir; look – with a big parcel."

"No – that's not the men," said Philip. "Is it, Mary? Our men had different clothes – one was in a brown suit with a brown tie, and the other was in a green jacket with a black tie."

"Right. Go on again, sir, please," said the policeman. "Ah, wait – what about

these men coming round the corner
with a case?"

The men had on the right-coloured
suits, but they were not a bit like the
ones the children had seen.

"No – both those men are small," said
Mary, "and our men are tall. One had a
little moustache and the other hadn't.
And they both wore hats like Daddy's,
and one man had a tiny feather stuck
into his hat-band."

"My word – these kids of yours notice
a lot, don't they?" said the policeman,
most impressed. "They'll be telling us
how many toes the men had next!"

The children laughed. They were
keeping a very close look-out indeed.
They had felt so ashamed of letting
those men steal their father's case
under their very noses; now they felt
they really must catch them and get the
case back, or they would never forgive
themselves.

Up the hill and down. No men at all.
Round the town and back again. Plenty
of men, but not the ones they wanted.

"Of course they might have gone into a shop somewhere, or the cinema," said the policeman. "They've had time to get a good way away now, and unless they caught a bus or a train they'll probably be sitting down having tea somewhere – or seeing a film. I'm afraid we'll have to give up finding them this way, sir. I've got all particulars from the children – though I'd like to ask them a few questions – and we'll send out descriptions of the men everywhere."

"Right," said Dr Fenton. "Well, would you like to come along to my house and ask the children what else you want to know?"

Mary spoke up in a very small voice:

"Daddy, I suppose we don't deserve those ice-creams now, do we?"

"Bless us all!" said Daddy. "I'd quite forgotten we were going to have some. Yes, of course we'll have them. Constable, will you join us? You can ask your questions in the bakery."

"Yes, sir. It would be quite a treat," said the policeman, beaming round at the two children. "It's a long time since I was taken to have an ice-cream."

They came to the bakery, and they got out. This time Daddy locked his car well and truly. "Though it's rather like locking the stable door after the horse has gone," he told the children. "Come along."

They went into the tea-room of the bakery, but it was tea-time now and the place was full. "I've a little room upstairs," said the shop-woman. "I think there's a table up there, sir."

So up they went and found the table. A girl came to take their order. Whilst they were waiting for their ice-creams

the two children looked round the room. They had never been in this little room before, and they didn't think it was as nice as the big one downstairs. Still, the ice-creams would be just as good!

Mary suddenly trod hard on Philip's toe. Philip looked at her in surprise. Then he looked where she was looking, and he went bright red with excitement.

Sitting huddled together in the darkest corner of the little room were the two men who had stolen their father's case! There was no mistaking them at all – one with a little moustache, one with none; one with a

green jacket and black tie, and the other in brown with a brown tie.

And under the table was a very large suitcase! The children looked at one another. They didn't dare to whisper their news in case the men suspected something. So Philip took out his little notebook and pencil and scribbled something in it. He passed it silently to his father.

"Those are the men over there. Look at the suitcase under the table!" That was what he had written.

His father passed the note to the policeman, who looked casually over at the two men. He in turn scribbled a note very quickly and had it ready for

403

the girl when she came with their ice-creams. His note was short and clear.

"Take this to the police-station," was written on the outside. And inside: *"Send two men to Harrison's Bakery at once. Upstairs. Johns."*

The girl brought their ice-creams, took the note, looked at the outside, seemed very scared, and went out quickly. Two other people finished their tea and went. That left only the two men and the children's table.

The girl came back and slid a note into the policeman's hands. One of the two men called out to her.

"Hey, miss – what times does the bus to Highlands go?"

"Not for fifteen minutes, sir," said the girl.

"Good," thought the children. "The men won't slip out yet."

Two strange men came into the tea-room and sat down silently at the table next to the children's. They nodded to the policeman, who at once got up and went over to the two men.

"I have reason to think that there is stolen property in that case of yours," he said. "Will you open it?"

The men leapt up at once, blustering angrily. One caught up the case. "What cheek!" he said. "Who are you to say things like that! I'll report you to the police."

"I *am* the police," said the policeman stolidly. "Open that case, please."

The men pushed him aside and went to the door. But the other two policemen were there now. No escape that way!

"Huh! Three of you!" said one of the men in disgust. "All right. Open the case. Though how you know it was us

405

that did the job I don't know. There wasn't anyone to see."

"Walls have ears," said the policeman, opening the case and taking out Dr Fenton's bag from inside. "And hedges have eyes!"

Well, of course, the two men had no idea what he was talking about, but the children knew! They were pleased to see the two men marched off.

"I'm glad you've got your bag back, Daddy," said Mary. "We were silly to let it be stolen. What a good thing we came here for ice-creams!"

"It was," said Daddy. "I say – what about another one each just to celebrate your exciting adventure!"

A Visitor
to Dinner

Keith and Penny were very fond of the birds. In the spring they put out lucky-bags for them – net bags full of dead leaves, moss, hair and feathers so that the birds could come and take what they wanted for their nests. In the summer they put out bowls of water for the birds to bathe in and drink.

And when the cold weather came they had a bird-table, of course. Keith had made it himself.

"I think it's a very good table, Keith," said Penny. "I know it's only a flat bit of wood nailed on top of a pole, with twigs nailed at the back for the birds to perch on when they fly down – but you've made it very strongly, and the birds really do love it."

So they did. The sparrows were always there, of course. The robin came by himself, and wouldn't let any other robin near the table. The blackbirds came and the thrushes, and the little chaffinches flew down to it a dozen times a day.

"There are always plenty of guests at your table!" Mother said to them. "Whenever I look out of the window I see some bird or other pecking away there."

"Yes – and the robin still likes to bathe in the little dish of water," said Penny, "although the winter is here and the days are cold. He splashes in the water as if it were summer!"

So he did – and the thrush sometimes had a bathe too, though he was really too big for the little dish. The children were always thinking of things to put on their bird-table for

their visitors to eat. They really were very good friends to them.

They put out all the crumbs, of course, and the scrapings from every pudding. They put out the skins of potatoes that had been boiled in their jackets, and once a week Mother baked two potatoes specially for the birds. Keith and Penny cut them in half, let them cool, and then put the four halves on the table.

"You should see the birds fight for the potato, Mother!" said Penny. "They simply love it. Have you a bone we can have for the starlings? They were down there on the table today, and they do so like a bone."

So Mother gave them a bone and the starlings flew down and squabbled over it as they always did. They called each other rude names and pushed one

409

another off the bone. They really were very funny.

"What birds come to your table?" asked Daddy, one evening. "Anything exciting? When I kept a table a nut-hatch once came to it for nuts I put there – he was a beauty. He whistled as the paper-boy does."

"Did he really?" said Penny. "I wish we had some uncommon bird visitors – but we never do. We get the sparrows and chaffinches, the blackbirds and thrushes, the robins and the starlings."

"And the tits," said Keith. "Don't

forget them. We hung a piece of fat meat on a bit of string yesterday, Daddy, and the blue tits came and swung on the string like acrobats!"

"But one tit was the cleverest of the lot," said Penny. "He stood on the edge of the table and hauled the fat up to him! I could hardly believe my eyes."

"Very clever," said Daddy. "But those are all quite common birds. Perhaps one of these days you will get a rare one."

All the birds in that district knew Keith and Penny, and their bird-table. The sparrows chattered about them, the chaffinches told the two bullfinches that lived in the hedgerow, and tried to make them come to the table, and the song-thrush told his big cousin, the mistlethrush.

"I'll come to the children's table after Christmas," said the mistle-thrush. "Perhaps they will put out their mistletoe sprays for me then, and I can peck off the mistletoe berries. I do like them so much."

Then one day a ripple of excitement ran through the bird-world in that district. "Have you seen the Big-Beaked One? Have you seen him? He is enormous!"

Sparrows told the news to chaffinches, blackbirds called to peewits up in the sky, and the peewits told the rooks and jackdaws.

"There's a great bird in the fields – he's called the Big-Beaked One!" all the birds cried. "Nobody knows where he comes from."

"What does he eat?" called the kingfisher.

"He's like you – he wants fish," said the blackbird. "But he says the little fish you catch are no use to him – he wants big fish to fill his beak!"

The birds went to see this strange visitor. They stared at him in awe. Truly he was big and truly he had a big beak – an enormous one, which would surely take twenty fish at a time! The big bird was not very friendly. He would not say where he had come from nor what his real name was. He sat by the riverside where the kingfisher fished, and grumbled because the fish were so small.

"I am hungry," he said. "I am always hungry. Are you not hungry too, thrushes, blackbirds and sparrows?"

"No," piped up a sparrow, "we know where there is always a table spread with good things for us."

Big-Beaked One listened hard. "A table spread with good things?" he said. "Is there fish?"

"I've never seen any," said the sparrow. "But Keith and Penny, the two children who always spread the table for us each day, will be sure to get

413

you fish if you want some. They are very, very kind."

"Then show me where this table is," said Big-Beaked One, and he flapped his great wings and made such a wind that the sparrow was blown right off his twig.

It was the blackbird who took him to the table. "There you are," he said. "I'm afraid the table is not large enough for a bird like you – but if you sit right in the middle of it you'll have room."

And that afternoon for the first time Keith and Penny caught sight of the strange and unexpected visitor! They stared in the greatest astonishment.

"Are we dreaming?" said Keith. "Can you see a most enormous bird on

414

our table, Penny?"

"Yes – and oh, Keith – it looks like a
pelican to me!" said Penny, amazed.

"A pelican – why, I believe you are
right!" said Keith. "He's certainly got a
pelican's funny beak – very big indeed,
with a pouch to hold fish. But where
has he come from?"

"There aren't any pelicans in *this*
country," said Penny. "Are we
dreaming?"

"No. That bird looks much too real
for a dream," said Keith. "It *is* a
pelican! Why has it come?"

"For us to feed it, of course," said
Penny. "I expect it's hungry, poor
thing, and the other birds have told it
to come to our table. We must give it
food."

"Yes – that's all very well – but it
won't eat bread or cake or anything
like that," said Keith. "Pelicans live on
fish!"

"Then we'll go and buy some fish
from the fishmonger's," said Penny.
"That's easy. I'll go and tell Mother

415

and ask her for some money."

But Mother was out. So the children took their own money-boxes and emptied them. They looked doubtfully at the money. "Do you think it's enough?" said Penny. "The pelican looks as if it could eat up an awful lot of fish."

"It'll have to be enough," said Keith. "It's all we've got. Come on, we'd better go and buy the fish before the pelican gets tired of waiting."

Penny called out of the window. "Pelican! Welcome to our bird-table. We're sorry there's no fish, but we didn't know you were coming. We're just going to get some for you!"

The pelican looked at them out of his artful-looking eyes. He nodded his head slowly. "There! I'm sure he understood," said Penny. The children ran to their front gate and down the road. They were soon at the fishmonger's.

"What fish do you want?" asked the man.

416

"Have you anything fit for pelicans?" asked Keith.

The fishmonger laughed.

"Don't be funny," he said. "I'm busy. What fish do you want? And don't tell me you want something for an ostrich this time."

"No, we don't," said Penny. "It really is for a pelican."

The fishmonger lost patience with them. "I've no time to joke about pelicans," he said. "Here, take some herrings. I've got plenty of those."

The pelican was still on their table, waiting patiently. "I wonder if he'll take them from us," said Keith. He held out a herring and the pelican snapped at it at once! It took one from

417

Penny next.

"Isn't he tame?" said Keith. "What will Daddy say when we tell him we had a pelican visitor this afternoon?"

Well, Daddy simply didn't believe it, of course. He laughed. "Don't try to kid me with pelican tales," he said. "I'll believe in the pelican when I see him!"

"You'll see him tomorrow, perhaps," said Penny. "He liked the fish we gave him today, so I expect he'll come back."

Well, he did! He arrived the very next morning and sat solidly in the middle of the bird-table, waiting, much to the annoyance of the sparrows and other small birds who hadn't any room to perch at all!

"There he is, Daddy – *now* will you believe us?" asked Keith. Daddy went to the window. He stared in silence. Then he spoke in surprise.

"Well! It is a pelican. He's escaped from somewhere, of course. Perhaps from the Zoo. I'll ring them up and see."

418

So he rang up the Zoo – and they said yes, Percy the Pelican had escaped. Was he *really* on the children's bird-table?

"Yes. The children are giving him fish," said Daddy. "Can you send a keeper down? I think you could catch him easily if he visits us again."

That afternoon a keeper arrived from the Zoo. He carried a big long- handled net with him. He hid behind a bush and waited.

When Percy flew down, the children went to the table to give him fish – and down over him came the keeper's net. He was caught!

The keeper took him back to the Zoo. The children were very sorry, because they liked Percy. "All the same he would have been expensive to feed," said Penny. "We've already spent all the money we've saved up for Mummy's birthday, worse luck!" But that didn't matter after all – because by the next day's post there came a letter from the Zoo – and in it was five pounds for Keith and five pounds for Penny.

"Just to pay for Percy's board and lodging," said the note.

"We'll *never* have such an unusual visitor again," said Keith. "Fancy having Percy the Pelican to dinner! I'm sure nobody else ever has."

But I'd like to. Wouldn't you?

Look Out for the Elephant!

"There's an elephant loose!" shouted Jim, rushing into the school playground. "I just heard a man say so. It's escaped from the circus."

"Where is it, where is it?" cried all the children, rushing round Jim.

"It's in the park – and they're afraid it will trample down all the lovely flowers," said Jim.

"Oh, what a shame!" said Sara. She loved flowers, and she couldn't bear to think of the elephant's great feet trampling and breaking them all.

"They've sent for men with sticks," said Jim. "They'll scare that bad elephant properly. I wouldn't mind chasing him myself."

"But elephants are *nice*," said Sara.

"I rode on one heaps of times at the zoo. They are gentle and kind. They can't help being big and having enormous feet. I think it's horrid to send for men with sticks!"

"All right, then – *you* go and get the elephant out of the park!" said Jim scornfully. "Go on! See if it will come and eat out of your hand and follow you like a dog! I tell you, big sticks are the only thing to frighten an elephant!"

Sara stood listening to Jim. She was just about to tell him that an elephant *had* eaten out of her hand at the zoo when she had given him a bun – and then a grand idea came into her head!

Now when Sara had an idea she always acted on it at once. So she turned and ran over to the baker's. She bought twelve buns out of her pocket money and put them into her school satchel.

You can guess what her idea was now, can't you? Well, well – whoever would think of such a thing? Only Sara!

She ran down the street and made for the park. It wasn't very far away. There was a place in the hedge she could get through. She squeezed through it, and there she was in the park. Where was the elephant?

Well, he wasn't very difficult to see, as you can imagine. There he stood, waving his enormous trunk to and fro, his great feet very near to a big bed of glorious dahlias.

In the distance Sara could hear shouting, and she guessed that men were coming with sticks.

"They'll only scare him and he'll go

423

galloping over the dahlias," thought Sara. "I'd better hurry."

So she trotted down the path to where the big elephant stood. She went right up to him.

"You're awfully like the elephant who gave me rides at the zoo," she told him, and he looked down at her out of little, twinkling eyes. He flapped his ears and made a little trumpeting noise.

"Are you asking for a bun?" said Sara, and she put her hand in her satchel. "Well, here's one."

The elephant put out his trunk and took the bun. He swung his trunk up

to his big mouth – and the bun was gone! He held out his trunk for another.

"Well, you can have all my buns if you come quietly down this path with me," said Sara, "away from these lovely flower-beds. Your feet are so big, you know. Here you are, here's another bun."

She gave him another, and then began to walk down the path to the park gate. The elephant, seeing that she had plenty more buns, followed her closely, trying to put his trunk inside the satchel.

Sara laughed. "Oh, you wait until I give you one! There you are. Now do come along. We'll soon be at the gate!

Well, well, well! The men with sticks stopped at once when they saw the elephant following little Sara like a dog.

"Look at that!" they said. "That kid has got old Jumbo eating out of her hand! Send his keeper to that park gate – that will be the place to capture the

425

elephant. He's not scared any more, or angry. Well, would you believe it!"

Jumbo followed Sara all the way to the gate, eating the buns she gave him – and there at the gate was the elephant's keeper waiting for him! Jumbo was very glad indeed to see him. He loved his keeper.

"Thank you, little girl," said the keeper gratefully. "If it hadn't been for you, poor Jumbo would have been sent racing all over the flower-beds in fright, and he might have done a lot of damage. Now – is there any reward you'd like for getting him to come quietly?"

"Well," said Sara, "I suppose – I suppose I couldn't ride on his head, could I, right past our school? The children would hardly believe it if they

426

saw me there!"

"Yes. Old Jumbo will set you on his head and hold you there with his trunk," said the keeper with a laugh. "Hup, Jumbo, hup!"

Jumbo picked up Sara very gently and set her on his big head. Then, holding her there with his trunk, he set off down the road that led past the school, swaying this way and that.

"Look! LOOK! It's Sara up there!" shouted the children. "Hurrah for Sara! Sara, how did you get there? Oh, SARA!"

It was a lovely reward, wasn't it? She deserved it, though, because she really did have a very good idea!

427

Caterpillars' Party

The big moth sailed down to where the five caterpillars were busy eating their dinner. They were fat caterpillars, each with a fur coat on, and they ate very fast indeed.

"Hallo!" said the big moth. "We moths are giving a party for you caterpillars tomorrow night. Would you like to come?"

"A party!" said the biggest caterpillar. "Yes, of course we'd like to come, but why are you giving a party for *us*?"

"Well," said the moth, waving his beautiful feelers about. "I don't expect you know it, but one day *you* will be moths like us! And we thought we would give a party for you, and tell you

428

how to behave when the time comes for you to be moths."

The furry caterpillars were astonished. "How can we change into moths?" they said. "We have no wings. We are covered with fur. We are quite different from you!"

"I dare say!" said the moth. "But all the same, my words will come true. You see if they don't! Well, what about this party?"

"We'd love to come!" said the caterpillars at once.

"Well, come to the big bush over there tomorrow night when the moon is full," said the moth. "Look out for

the hedgehog, though, if he's about. He likes a meal of grubs as fat as you!"

Off flew the moth, his powdery wings taking him high in the air. He was a beautiful thing. The caterpillars watched him go. Could it be true that one day they would be as lovely as that, and fly through the air?

A small pixie came wandering by. The caterpillars called to him eagerly. "Tippy! We're going to a party!"

"Really?" said Tippy. "Well, mind you go nice and clean, with your coats gleaming. Everyone has to look his best at a party."

He skipped off. The caterpillars looked at one another. "Do we look nice enough to go to a party? Ought we to dress ourselves up or something? The moths do look so beautiful."

Now that night there came a great rainstorm. The enormous raindrops

battered the plants on which the caterpillars fed, and broke them. The frightened creatures found themselves on the ground in the mud. They squirmed here and there, but they couldn't get away from the rain.

"What a mess we are in!" said one, sadly. "All covered with mud – and our fur dirty and wet. We can't possibly go to the party."

They looked at one another. They certainly were in a dreadful mess. No party for them! Why, the moths would turn them away in disgust.

And just then who should come by again but Tippy the pixie. They called to him dolefully. "Tippy! See what the rain has done to us! We can't go to the party."

431

Tippy looked at the wet, muddy, untidy caterpillars. He scratched his head and thought hard. Then he spoke. "Caterpillars, I could clean you and tidy you up, if you like – but you would have to give me a reward."

"Just say what you would like and if we can give it to you, you shall have it," said the caterpillars eagerly. "But don't ask for gold, because we don't even know what it is, unless it is the sunshine that shines each day, and you have plenty of that yourself."

"I'll tell you what I want," said Tippy. "I want your fur coats! I could clean them, and make them into fur rugs to sell to the pixies to put on their beds in the winter-time."

There was a most astonished silence. Then the biggest caterpillar spoke in a shocked voice. "What! Give you the fur coats we wear? Why, they *grow* on us! We couldn't possibly do that."

Tippy grinned. "Well, listen – suppose a time comes when you really don't want your hairy coats – when

432

you want to throw them away – will you give them to me then? I promise not to ask you for them unless you say you don't want them."

"All right," said the biggest caterpillar, cheering up. "That's a bargain. You get us all nice and tidy for the party – and we'll let you have our fur coats if we don't want them."

So Tippy set to work on the hairy caterpillars. He fetched his little sponge. He dipped it into a little pool of dew and wetted it. Then he sponged

433

each muddy caterpillar very carefully to get off the mud. Soon their fur coats were quite clean again.

"Now you are very wet," said Tippy. "Sit out here in the sun – it's just rising, look – and see if you can get really warm and dry."

So out they all sat. Tippy watched them. Then he fetched his little brush, and began to brush the caterpillars' soft, dry hairs.

"Beautiful!" said Tippy, brushing away hard. "It's a pity there's no time to curl your hairs a bit. You'd look fine. There now – that's the last one of you done. Your fur coats have never looked nicer. Stay in the sun today, and towards evening I'll give you one more brushing."

When the caterpillars went to the

moth's party they looked very neat and tidy indeed. Tippy had even parted their hairs down the middle, and squirted a little of his best scent on them. The moths thought they looked very fine indeed.

The party was lovely. There was plenty to eat, and the dew-drinks were all flavoured with honey that the moths had drawn from flowers with their long tongues. They told the caterpillars many interesting things, half of which the long-bodied creatures could not believe.

435

"They said we would go to sleep for a long time and wake up as moths," said the fattest caterpillar, on his way home. "What nonsense!"

"And they said that although we should go to sleep as caterpillars, with heaps of legs, a long body, and no wings, we should wake up with only six legs, some fine feelers, a short body, and two pairs of wings!" said another caterpillar. "Impossible! Such things don't happen."

They told all these things to Tippy when they next saw him. He laughed.

"Well, you never know," he said. "There is plenty of most peculiar magic in the world, you know. But before you go to sleep, and change into moths, I want those fur coats of yours! It's about time I had them, too. You eat so much, caterpillars, that I am sure you will burst your skins soon!"

The caterpillars certainly were eating a lot – and some of them were so fat they looked as if they might burst at any moment. Then the biggest one

436

suddenly stopped eating.

"I feel strange," he said. "Very strange. My skin is too tight for me. It's splitting! It is, really!"

Pop! It split down his back. "I must get out of my skin!" cried the caterpillar. "It's too tight. It's too tight! Help me, Tippy!"

Tippy helped him. The caterpillar wriggled and Tippy tugged. Soon the tight skin was peeling away from the caterpillar's body. It was off! There it lay beside him, a little ball of fur, a tiny fur-coat that he no longer wanted.

"You've got a beautiful new hairy

437

skin underneath!" said all the other caterpillars, staring. "What a wonderful thing!"

"Of course he has!" said Tippy. "I've seen caterpillars doing this for years! Hurry up and split your coats, you others. I want the skins to make into fur rugs. Don't forget your bargain with me."

Well, of course, the other caterpillars soon got so fat that their skins split too, and you should have seen Tippy pulling and tugging at them, and the caterpillars wriggling. Soon the pixie had a fine hoard of furry skins in his cottage. The caterpillars were only too pleased to let him have them. They all had beautiful new furry coats, under their old skins!

And dear me, those coats split too as

soon as the caterpillars grew too fat for them! Tippy was always there when that happened, you may be sure, and he rolled up the cast-off fur coats, put them on his shoulder, and marched off with them.

One day the caterpillars could eat no more. They began to weave themselves silken beds, and they went to sleep inside these. They were too sleepy even to say goodbye to Tippy.

But he said goodbye to them. "I'll see you when you wake up!" he said. "And you'll see what a fine little shop I have then, with fur rugs of all kinds hanging up for sale!"

He was soon very busy. He cut each

439

furry coat and trimmed it so that it made an oblong rug. He washed each one carefully and set it to dry in the sun. Then he brushed the fur well.

After that he hired a tiny shop and hung up the rugs for sale. The very small ones were for the pixie cots or prams. The bigger ones were for beds. And how the little folk hurried to buy them!

"Such beautiful rugs! As warm as can be! Wherever did Tippy get them? Tippy dear, what fur is this? What animal gave you his skin for these lovely rugs?"

But Tippy wouldn't tell his secret. No, he wasn't going to have anyone sharing such a fine secret!

One day the caterpillars in the silken cocoons woke up. They crawled out of their cosy beds and looked round. They stared at one another in surprise.

"We're different! We've got wings! We're moths!"

So they were. They spread their soft, powdery wings and flew off into the

440

night air, rejoicing. It had been nice to be greedy caterpillars – but oh, how much nicer to be moths, with wings like the little folks, and with a long tongue that could pierce to the heart of a flower and drink the sweet nectar hidden there!

They went to see Tippy. He showed them his fine collection of fur rugs. "See?" he said. "You didn't want them but I did! They will keep many a pixie and elf warm in the winter nights. How different you look, moths! Magic

441

has been at work on you – powerful magic!"

It's strange, isn't it, that caterpillars throw away their coats when they grow too big for them? Have you ever found one, rolled up and cast away? Perhaps Tippy has been before you and taken each one. Clever little thing, isn't he?

Untidy William

There was once a boy who was very untidy. His name was William, and his mother was always scolding him for being so untidy.

"You never put *any*thing away, William!" she would say. "You leave your shoes out – you leave your cap on the floor – you throw your coat down. It's simply dreadful."

"Sorry, Mother!" said William cheerfully.

"You're *not* sorry!" said his mother. "If you were, you would try to do better. I am always clearing up after you – and yet you never try to help me."

"Well, I *will* try!" said William. So the next day he really tried. He hung up his cap on the peg, and he put his shoes into

the cupboard. Gracious, he did feel good! But as he dropped his coat on the floor and left his scarf on the stairs, he didn't really do very well after all!

He went upstairs. He opened the desk he had there, to find a favourite pencil. He couldn't find it, so he scrabbled about in the desk just as if he were a dog scratching in the ground for a hidden bone – and, of course, everything went flying out of his desk on to the floor!

Did William pick them up? Of course not! Hadn't he hung up his cap on the peg and put his shoes away in the cupboard? Well, that was tidiness enough for one day, as far as William was concerned.

Then William sat down on the clean bedcover and creased that. He knocked his pyjamas on to the floor and didn't pick them up. His mother came in to speak to him and saw the untidy mess in his bedroom.

"William! I thought you were going to try and be really tidy today!" she said. "And you seem to be worse than ever!"

"Well, Mother, I like that!" said William. "Didn't you see how I had hung up my cap on its peg, and put my shoes away in the cupboard? I do think you might have noticed that!"

"All I noticed was that your coat was on the floor in the hall, and I tripped over your scarf as I came upstairs!" said his mother. "William, I don't know what to do with you."

She went out of the room. William sat and thought for a minute. Then he got up.

"I've often read in stories that people can get spells from the fairy-folk to put things right when they are untidy and untruthful or greedy," he thought. "I've a good mind to go to old Dame Goody and ask her if she knows of one to keep me tidy. Then I wouldn't keep getting into trouble with Mother. It would be so nice to be tidy without having to keep on remembering it."

He put on his outdoor things and went up the hill to where old Dame Goody lived. She was a funny little old lady, and

446

she had most peculiar eyes. Sometimes they looked grey and sometimes they looked green. That was because her grandmother had been first cousin to a fairy.

Well, Dame Goody was surprised to see William, for usually the children were rather afraid of her, though she was a kind old lady, who wouldn't have hurt anybody for anything.

"Good morning, Dame Goody," said William. "I expect you know that I'm awfully untidy, don't you?"

"Well, I can see it," said the old woman, looking down at William's shoes, which were both undone, and at his coat, which had the buttons done up wrongly.

"Do you think you could possibly give me a spell to make me tidy without my bothering much about it?" asked William. "I would so much like one. I could pay you for it. I've got fifty pence in my money-box."

"Well, I believe I *have* got an old, old spell tucked away somewhere that my

447

grandmother had by her," said Dame
Goody, her eyes suddenly looking very
green. "And if it would do for a tidy-
spell, you can have it for fifty pence."

She went off into the back room, and
William heard her hunting in drawers
for the old, old spell. At last she came
back, smiling. She held a funny little tin
in her hand. It was bright blue, and at
the top it had a head instead of a lid.

"I've found the spell," said Dame
Goody. "I'll scatter it over you, and you
will then find that your things will all
be terribly tidy!"

"But *I* want to be tidy," said William,
"not my things."

"Well, it's easier to make your things
tidy than you," said Dame Goody. "Now
stand still, please!"

William stood still. Dame Goody took off the funny little wooden head that was on the top of the tin instead of a lid, and scattered a blue powder all over William.

"I feel as if you are peppering me!" said William, beginning to sneeze. "A-tish-oo!"

Dame Goody muttered a string of magic words that sounded very strange to William. Then she clapped the lid on to the tin, and nodded her head at him.

"The spell will work tomorrow morning," she said. "I hope it's all right. It's rather old, you see. It may have gone a bit wrong."

449

"What should it do?" asked William.

"Well, it should make anything belonging to you put itself neatly away," said Dame Goody. "Your pencils should put themselves away in the box. Your cap should hang itself up on the peg. Your clothes should fold themselves up neatly when you take them off, and put themselves on a chair or away in a drawer."

"That sounds marvellous!" said William, pleased. "Thank you, Dame Goody. I shall now be known as the tidiest boy in the country!" He went off, smiling, wishing that the next day would come quickly.

It came. William awoke, dressed himself, and then threw down his pyjamas on the floor on purpose to see if the spell was working.

And do you know, those pyjamas solemnly got up, folded themselves neatly, and put themselves into the pyjama-case on the bed. It was most extraordinary to watch them.

"This is great!" thought William.

"Simply great!"

He threw his toothbrush on to the floor. It at once flew up into the air, and settled itself calmly into the tooth mug. William was very pleased indeed.

He went downstairs, in good time for breakfast. His father was there, reading the newspaper, and he looked up as William came in. "Hallo, son," he said, and then buried himself behind the paper again. "Sit down and get on with your porridge," his mother called from the kitchen. "I'm just getting the bacon and eggs!"

William sat down. He was just about to put sugar on his porridge, when something most peculiar happened. His shoes came off, and his socks unpeeled from his legs!

William looked down in astonishment. Whatever could be happening? To his enormous surprise he saw his shoes hopping neatly together over the floor. They went out of the door, and he heard them going to the hall-cupboard! Well, well, well!

His socks rolled themselves into a neat ball, and then bowled themselves out of the door too. They went upstairs and put themselves into a drawer.

Then William's jacket took itself off William and flew away to hang itself up. His shirt and tie came off and his shorts. They all folded themselves up very neatly indeed and then went upstairs to put themselves away.

452

And there was William sitting at the breakfast table in his vest! He simply didn't know what to do.

"My goodness! The spell *has* gone wrong!" he thought in dismay. "Instead of waiting until I was untidy, my things have put themselves away now! I'd better creep upstairs before anyone sees me and dress again."

Well, William was just about to creep away when his mother came into the room with the bacon and eggs. She saw William sitting at the table in his vest and she almost dropped the dish in amazement.

453

"*William!* Why haven't you dressed? Don't you know that you are only in your vest? Really, is this the way to come down to breakfast? What in the world are you thinking of?"

Daddy looked up in surprise. How he stared when he saw poor William in nothing but his vest!

"Is this a joke?" he asked. "Because, if so, I don't think it is at all amusing! Boys who come down in their vests ought to be punished."

William fled upstairs. Goodness, this was dreadful! He didn't like it at all!

William found his things in the drawers and in his cupboard and dressed himself again. He tied his shoelaces firmly in a knot, in case his shoes thought of hopping off again. He did up all his buttons tightly.

"It would be simply dreadful if they all came off again," he thought. "I really

don't know what Daddy would say!"

Well, nothing happened at breakfast-time except that a spoon which William dropped, hopped up to the table again on its own, and put itself neatly by William's plate.

"Now that's good," thought William. "That's the sort of thing that I wanted the spell for. If only it goes on working like that, it will be fine."

But it didn't! William put on his cap, jacket, scarf, and gloves, and went to

455

catch the bus to go to school. And in the bus, his cap, jacket, scarf, and gloves all undid themselves, and sailed away out of the bus door! They fled home, hung themselves up, or put themselves in a drawer – and there was poor cold William shivering in the bus without any of his outdoor clothes! There was only an old man in the bus besides William. The conductor was on the top of the bus. The old man was rather astonished to see William without any cap or coat, but he said nothing.

But Mr Brown, his teacher, said quite a lot. "William! How is it that you have come to school like this? Really, what are you thinking of to come without your cap or jacket? You will catch a dreadful cold on this bitter winter day!"

William couldn't say that his things had flown away by themselves, so he said nothing. He went into his classroom and sat down.

And immediately all the pencils, rubber, and pocket-knife in his pocket hopped out to the desk and put themselves tidily into his box! Mr Brown heard the noise and looked up.

"Is it really necessary to make all that noise with your pencil-box, William?" he asked. William said he was sorry, and glared at his pencils and rubber and knife. His pencil-box lid shut down with a snap.

And then the books on William's desk decided that the right place for them was the bookcase! So they took a jump and landed on the bookshelf with a crash. Everyone looked up.

"William! Did *you* throw your books on to the shelf?" asked Mr Brown. "What

457

can be the matter with you today?"

"I didn't throw them," said William.

"Well, I suppose you will tell me that they jumped there themselves!" said Mr Brown.

"That's just what they did do," said poor William.

"Any more of this behaviour and you will stay in at the end of the morning," said Mr Brown sternly.

William looked worried. He did hope that the spell wouldn't work any more that morning! Oh, why had he ever tried to get a tidy-spell? It was getting him into great difficulties.

After playtime that morning, the children settled down to a history lesson. Mr Brown was teaching them about the people of long ago. William listened well, for he loved history stories.

And then he felt his right shoe twisting about on his foot! The spell was beginning to work again. The shoe wanted to take itself home and put itself away into the cupboard. But

William had tied the laces very tightly and it couldn't get itself off!

William tried to keep his foot still – but the spell worked very hard, and the shoe twisted about so much that it twisted William's foot with it.

"William! Is it *you* fidgeting?" cried Mr Brown at last. "Keep your feet still!"

But that was just what William couldn't do! The spell began to work in both shoes, and so both William's feet began to fidget about. Mr Brown was very cross.

"Stand up, William," he said. "If you can't *sit* still, perhaps you can stand still!"

So William had to stand for the rest of the history lesson, and he didn't like

459

it at all. His shoes twisted about for a while, then grew tired and stopped.

At the end of the morning came a lesson that William liked very much. It was woodwork. William was making a ship. He had a hammer, screwdriver, chisel, pincers, gimlet, and nails of his own. He went with the other boys to get his tools from the woodwork cupboard.

Well, the spell began to work again as soon as William was happily hammering nails into his ship. He put down his tools for a moment and took up his ship to ask Mr Brown if it was all right. And when he came back to his desk, his tools had disappeared!

"Who's taken my tools?" asked

William, looking all round. Nobody had! It was very mysterious. Then William wondered if the spell was working again. Perhaps his tools had put themselves away in the box in the woodwork cupboard. So he went to look – and sure enough, there they were! William took them out, whilst all the boys looked on in astonishment.

"Why did you put them away in the middle of the lesson?" asked Dick.

William didn't answer. He didn't know what to say. He set to work again.

Then he went to look at a submarine that another boy was making, and when he got back to his own work – goodness gracious, his tools had disappeared *again!*

William knew where they were, of course – in the toolbox! So he went to get them again. Mr Brown looked up.

"William! Are you going to spend *all* the lesson in going to the cupboard and back for tools?" he asked.

Poor William! All he could say was, "Sorry, Mr Brown!" He was quite glad when the lesson came to an end.

Just as the children were lined up to be dismissed at half-past twelve, William felt his jacket coming undone. Goodness, were his clothes going to rush off again? No, no – he really couldn't bear it! William clutched his jacket to himself very tightly, and held it there.

"William! Have you got a pain or something?" asked Mr Brown in surprise. "Really, you are behaving in a funny manner today!"

William was glad to get outside – and

only just in time too! His jacket tore itself off him and flew down the road like a mad thing. Then his shoes and socks flew off too. William simply couldn't stop them. He stared in the greatest dismay.

The children shouted with laughter. "Look! The wind has blown away William's clothes! Oh, how funny!"

Poor old William! By the time he got home he had only his shorts and vest left, and he was very cold indeed. He crept in at the back door, hoping that his mother wouldn't notice him. He slipped upstairs. There, neatly hanging up, was his jacket. Folded tidily in the drawer was his shirt. His socks were rolled up in their drawer. His shoes were side by side by the bed.

"I simply can't stand this!" thought William, in despair. "I'm going to go to old Dame Goody at once and beg her to do something about this dreadful spell."

So he dressed himself again quickly and slipped out of the back door to go to old Dame Goody's. He banged loudly on her door and she opened it in surprise.

"Dame Goody! That spell worked all

wrong!" said William. "It's done the most dreadful things. Please do something about it."

"Dear me, I'm sorry," said Dame Goody. "Well, step inside a moment. I've got a special drink that stops spells from working if they are no longer needed. Now, where did I put it?"

She took what looked like a large-sized medicine bottle from a cupboard and poured out a drink for William. Gracious, it did taste horrid!

"Now, the spell won't work any more as long as you try to be tidy yourself," said Dame Goody. "It will only work if you are very untidy again. So I should be careful if I were you, William!"

"Goodness! I shall be the tidiest boy in the world!" said William, and he ran off home.

Well, he *isn't* the tidiest boy in the world, but he's a lot better. I watch him whenever I see him just in case I might suddenly see his tie whisk itself away or his cap fly off home to its peg. It really would be fun to see that, wouldn't it!

Freddie
Has a Job

Next door to Freddie there lived an old man who couldn't walk. He lay on a couch by his window all day long, and looked out into his garden. His name was Mr Still, and Freddie used to think it was a good name for anyone who had to lie still all day long.

The old man liked to see his flowers in the spring and summer. He had crocuses in the early spring, and then hundreds of golden daffodils nodding in the March wind. Then he had tulips, and after that a crowd of flowers – lupins, irises, sweet-williams, roses – everything you could think of.

He often smiled at Freddie when he saw him looking over the wall. "Good morning!" he would call. "A nice day for the roses – and for little boys too!"

When the autumn came, and all the flowers died except the big clumps of Michaelmas daisies, Mr Still got his housekeeper to put up a big bird-table. Then he watched that instead of his flowers. He used to have crumbs, seeds, soaked dog-biscuits, scrapings of pudding, and all kinds of things put on the table – and, dear me, you should have seen the number of birds that came to feast there!

Freddie could see the bird-table from his bedroom window. "Look, Mother!" he said each morning. "Look at all the sparrows – and there are two robins – and lots of greedy starlings – and a chaffinch and blackbird and a thrush."

It was fun to watch them all, but Mother wouldn't let him stay in his

cold bedroom for long. She made him come down to the warm sitting-room and play there. He couldn't see the bird-table from there.

"Mother, couldn't *I* have a bird-table too?" asked Freddie. "I would so love one."

"No, you can't," said Mother. "They are too expensive to buy, and I can't make one."

"I think *I* could," said Freddie. "All I want is a piece of flat wood for the top, and a long stick of some kind for the leg. That's all, Mother."

But Mother said no. And as she meant no when she said no, it wasn't any good asking her again.

Freddie watched the bird-table being taken down in the spring. Mr Still always said that he expected the birds to return his kindness then, and eat the greenfly and the caterpillars in his garden, so that his flowers would be as lovely as possible. The daffodils were beginning to flower. It was time for the birds to begin hunting for caterpillars!

The summer went by, and Mr Still's garden was more beautiful than ever – especially the roses; but when the autumn came, Freddie was most surprised to see that no bird-table was put up as usual! He looked from his bedroom window each morning as he dressed, but no – there was no bird-table there. Freddie wondered why.

So one morning he climbed up and sat on the wall between the two gardens. He called to Mr Still, who lay on his couch as usual by the window.

"Mr Still! Have you forgotten your bird-table this autumn? The birds come hopping round, looking for it, but you haven't had it put up."

Mr Still pushed open the window and nodded to Freddie. "No, I haven't

468

forgotten it," he said. "But you see, Freddie, things are difficult now, so every scrap of bread is used up, and I mustn't even buy dog-biscuits, because it is not right to give them to the birds when there is only just enough for our dogs. All the milk-puddings we have are scraped round for us to finish up ourselves, instead of giving them to the birds."

"Oh I see," said Freddie, sadly. "Mr Still, won't the birds be awfully disappointed? They keep looking for your bird-table, you know. Can't you put berries or seeds on it?"

"I could, if only my legs would take me into the fields and lanes to collect berries and wild seeds," said Mr Still. "But they won't walk, you know, Freddie. Something is wrong with them, and they can't be cured. I am just as disappointed as the birds about the bird-table – I did so love watching them. There isn't much for me to do here, and I do miss seeing my little feathered friends on the table."

"Well," said Freddie, suddenly thinking of a good idea, "well, Mr Still – let *me* be your legs! Why can't *I* go off into the fields and lanes and pick berries and seeds for the birds? Then you could have your table up, and watch the birds just as usual!"

"Would you really do that for me?" said Mr Still, smiling. "That's very kind of you indeed. If you would come to tea with me today I could tell you all the berries and seeds to get!"

So Freddie went to tea, and he and Mr Still talked about what to get for the bird-table. The next day was Saturday, so Freddie was able to go off to collect what he could find.

He did have fun. He found those lovely bright scarlet hips that grow on the wild rose. He found masses of

470

crimson hawthorn berries. He found purple privet berries, and plenty of yew berries too – though Mr Still said they were poisonous to little boys, so, although the birds loved them, Freddie mustn't eat them.

Freddie found plenty of seeds, too. He shook out old flower-heads into a paper bag, and tiny brown and black and yellow seeds rattled down into it from all kinds of plants.

"The birds will pick out those they want," said Mr Still. "They are very sensible. They know which are bad for them and which are good."

Freddie saw some great sunflower heads growing in Mrs Brown's garden one day. She was just cutting them down, and Freddie called to her.

"Mrs Brown! Do you want all those sunflower seeds for next year? If you don't, may I have some for a bird-table?"

"Certainly," said Mrs Brown. "I'll just keep one or two heads and dry them. I shall want seed for sunflowers again, because I do love these giant sunflowers – and I always save some seed for my sister's old parrot. But you can have all the other heads if you like!"

Wasn't Freddie pleased! There were seven big heads, full of fat sunflower seeds! He took them to Mr Still.

"Splendid!" said the old man. "We will dry them and then hang them up one by one from the bird-table, so that

the birds can peck them as they please.
They *will* have a feast!"

Freddie found acorns and chopped
them up to put on the bird-table. He
found hazelnuts and chopped those up
too, or threaded the shelled nuts on
string for the tits, who loved them.

"Well, really, I don't think I've ever
seen my bird-table so full before!" said
Mr Still, watching the crowd of birds
hopping on it. "It's marvellous. I don't
know what I should have done without
you, Freddie. I do hope you get some
pleasure out of watching the table,
too!"

"Well, I don't really see it much,
though I should simply love to," said
Freddie. "You see, I can only see it
from my window when I'm dressing. I
can't see it from downstairs. I do wish I

473

had one of my own – but Mother said no, and I can't bother her about it again."

"No, of course not,"said Mr Still. "Well, I can tell you I *have* had fun this winter watching the birds gobble up all the seeds and berries and nuts you have found for them."

The next week was Christmas week. Freddie was very busy making presents for everyone, and he hadn't much time to go hunting for berries and seeds – but it didn't matter, because he and Mr Still had a good store now, drying in a shed, ready to use if snow came and covered the trees and bushes.

Freddie gave Mr Still a present. It was a calendar he had made himself,

with a picture of two robins on it. Mr Still was very pleased indeed.

"Thank you," he said. "My present for you will be coming along soon. It may have two robins on it too, but I can't promise that!"

Freddie wondered what the present would be, and when Christmas morning came, he looked carefully through his presents to find Mr Still's. And he was very disappointed indeed not to find one! He thought Mr Still must have forgotten him after all.

But he hadn't – for when Freddie came downstairs and looked out of the window, what do you think he saw? He saw a fine big bird-table standing in his own garden, just near the window-sill, so that he could see it, and from it hung a large label that said, "For Freddie – from Mr Still and all the birds, with love and twitters and chirrups!"

"Oh!" cried Freddie joyfully. "A bird-table of my own! The finest one I've ever seen! Oh, Mother, I'm so happy!"

"You deserve to be, Freddie," said his mother, smiling at him. "And do look at your first visitors."

Sure enough, two robins flew down to the new bird-table and looked at Freddie as if to say, "Breakfast, please!" They were just like the ones on the calendar that Freddie had given to Mr Still. It was really very strange. He rushed in to tell Mr Still.

"Well, now you *will* be busy," said the old man, smiling. "You will have *two* bird-tables to spread each day with food and water. What a fine thing it was that you thought of going out to get berries and seeds!"

And don't forget, will you, that *you* can spread a bird-table with the same things, even if you have very few crumbs or potatoes or scrapings to spare. It's such fun hunting in the woods and fields for bird-food. You'll love it.